Murder
Simply Played

Rachael O. Phillips

Annie's®
AnniesFiction.com

Library of Congress-in-Publication Data
Murder Simply Played / by Rachael O. Phillips
p. cm.
I. Title

2016939736

AnniesFiction.com
(800) 282-6643
Amish Inn Mysteries™
Series Creator: Shari Lohner
Series Editors: Lorie Jones and Shari Lohner
Cover Illustrator: Kelley McMorris

10 11 12 13 14 | Printed in China | 9 8 7 6 5 4 3 2 1

1

Liz Eckardt took one look at Mary Ann Berne's orange-and-black cheerleading outfit and braced herself for an off-the-wall February morning. "What? Why?"

Unlocking her sewing shop's door in the rotunda of Liz's Olde Mansion Inn, Mary Ann looked better than anyone should at this hour, even if her clothing choice was questionable. The perfectly coiffed sixty-something set down a picnic basket and retrieved four giant, silvery pom-poms from one of the bins stacked on a nearby dolly. "Here you go." She tossed two pom-poms to Liz, who dropped them.

Mary Ann scooped them up and stuck them in Liz's hands, then raised her own pom-poms. "What you need is a good waker-upper. Let's do 'Two Bits.'"

Liz probed her groggy mind, still untouched by coffee. Wasn't *two bits* an old expression for twenty-five cents? Was her friend dressed like that for some sort of fund-raiser? What century was this again?

Shaking her pom-poms, Mary Ann pranced around Liz, bawling, "Two bits, four bits, six bits, a dollar, all for Pleasant Creek, stand up and holler!" She leaped, her still-supple figure contorting into a final flourish. "Yay!"

Startled out of her mind, Liz leaped higher and yelled louder. No flourish.

Fortunately, there was no fall either, though her fuzzy-socked feet slid Liz into a pirouette as if she were wearing skates. One leg of her comfy flannel pajama pants caught under her heel, pulling them lopsided down her hips.

Thank heaven no guests are around. Yanking her pants back up, Liz sagged against a wall. Too much noise. Too much flash from the pom-poms, Mary Ann's perfect silver hairdo, and her blinding smile and flawless teeth.

What possessed Mary Ann? Normally, she served as Sew Welcome's voice of reason. But this morning she'd totally lost it.

The grandfather clock chimed half past six. Liz's tired gaze fell on Beans the bulldog, comatose on his favorite rug near the front door. Somehow she'd inherited him when she bought the inn. Liz approached the motionless canine, trying to infuse some enthusiasm into her voice. "Here, boy. Time to go out."

Not even a whisker moved.

"Hey, it's not like I wanted to get up at the crack of dawn on a freezing morning either."

He lay as if part of the rug.

Though Liz knew Beans was the laziest dog on earth, she couldn't help kneeling beside him to make sure he was alive.

"He's all right," Mary Ann called, waving off Liz's obvious concern. "Beans is saving his strength; he knows what time of year it is."

The flicker of the dog's brown ear and his warm breath on Liz's hand assured her Beans was simply operating at his usual energy levels. But Mary Ann was making less sense with every passing moment. No explanation for the Halloween-hued cheerleader getup. And time of year? How about time of *day*?

"Fine. I don't mind staying inside." Liz hoisted herself to her feet and yawned. She walked back toward Mary Ann en route to the coffeemaker. "Any reason you decided to open the shop this early?"

"Oh, Sew Welcome won't open until the usual time." Mary Ann pushed the shop's heavy glass door and shoved the laden dolly through.

Liz rubbed her now-aching forehead. "New spring inventory?"

"Not yet." Mary Ann took the old-fashioned key from its lock, then moved the picnic basket from the foyer to the counter inside the store. "Just decorations I put up every year." She jerked a stepladder from a closet, unstacked the bins, and proceeded to yank off the top of each one.

Liz peered at the bizarre contents. Orange and black streamers and lots of orange-and-black stuffed owls with bared teeth. Teeth? Had she ever seen a bird with teeth?

Creepy.

"Is Sadie coming early to help?" Liz asked, referring to Mary Ann's lovable but eccentric partner, Sadie Schwarzentruber.

"No, she won't be coming." Mary Ann dived into another bin.

Liz cocked her head. Was that a secretive note in her friend's always forthright voice?

Mary Ann avoided her gaze as she rummaged through the bins. "Sadie doesn't help me with this."

"You bet she doesn't. Because it's not happening, Mary Ann Berne. Not in my shop."

Liz jumped as Sadie's fiery words peppered her from behind. *Can't. Turn. Around.* What if Sadie was wearing a red-and-green cheerleading outfit? What if she and Mary Ann performed "Two Bits" together?

A nightmare. That's what this is. Liz edged toward the door that led to her own apartment. *If I go back to bed, they'll disappear. I'll wake up in an hour and start this day over. With coffee.*

Sadie cut her escape short. "Liz, please tell this woman I don't want to see her stupid cheers this year. She hops like a teenybopper frog."

"Liz," Mary Ann huffed, "please tell *that* woman that *she* may have forgotten how to have fun, but I haven't."

Me? Tell them? *No way.* It was as if they'd exchanged personalities. Why were they drafting her to referee this predawn grandma smackdown?

Yet there was no sneaking away; they had her penned in. Liz took a deep breath and turned to Sadie.

Whew. No cheerleader uniform. However, she was breathing fire. Sadie didn't look the least inclined to do "Two Bits."

Nor did Mary Ann, dark eyes blazing.

What the heck had gotten into her friends? Liz said slowly, "You two are partners. You always work things out."

Sadie snapped, "Sure, when she has a brain. But when March Madness hits, her mind shuts down."

"March Madness?" Liz's brain shriveled further as the two threw verbal punches. *Isn't it only mid-February? Or did I hibernate for a few weeks?*

The last idea sounded ideal as Sadie and Mary Ann began a tug-of-war with the bins. Sadie re-covered them. Mary Ann tore the lids off. Undaunted, Sadie stacked them onto the dolly. Mary Ann knocked them over and dumped out the contents. Ignoring Liz's pleas, they raised their voices until she feared for the original leaded glass in her Victorian inn's windows.

When the air was filled with rancor and fuzzy bits from little stuffed orange-and-black owls, Liz dashed to the front door of the inn and hit the doorbell in desperation.

The chimes rang out as sweet and mannerly as Emily Post.

Both combatants stopped throwing owls and stared at Liz as she reentered the shop.

"What if someone dropped in?" A former attorney, she aimed her Lawyer Liz look at the women. "What would your friends and customers think if they saw you now?"

Mary Ann concentrated on her perfectly manicured nails. Sadie fiddled with a little owl's button eyes.

"I have no idea what you're really fighting about, but I refuse to believe that two lifelong friends and business partners can't resolve their differences like adults." Glancing at the picnic basket, Liz softened her tone. "I'll make coffee. You brought a pie, didn't you, Mary Ann?"

"Coconut cream."

"Ooh, Sadie's favorite. Sweet." *In more ways than one.* Liz's mouth watered.

"You planned to butter me up." Sadie put down the owl and lifted the basket's lid. With each sniff, her iron frown relaxed a little more.

"Sadie, please cut the pie before the room temperature melts it.

I'll pick up the owls." Mary Ann gathered several that had flown into the rotunda. Her cheeks had reddened, probably at the thought of Amish customers witnessing their immature conflict.

Liz stifled a smile as she and Sadie headed for the kitchen.

Sadie lost no time in relating her side of the story. Slicing the enormous pie topped with whipped cream, she confided, "Mary Ann's my best friend, but every February, she goes weird about the basketball team."

"Basketball team?" Liz turned from the coffeemaker.

"You definitely didn't grow up in Indiana." Sadie rolled her eyes. "Yes, basketball team. Not even a pro or college team. High school. And it's not just Mary Ann. The whole state goes bonkers every winter."

"You were fighting over high school basketball?" Liz had mediated numerous conflicts during her Boston law career, but none involved small-town gyms. Or cheerleaders.

"Don't look at me like that. I'm the sane person here."

Liz pilfered a little coffee from the still-brewing coffeemaker, downed it, and then said carefully, "Mary Ann doesn't really think she's a cheerleader, does she?"

Not Mary Ann, the shrewd businesswoman, the astute community leader, the mature influence when the Material Girls, their quilting group, got a little nuts.

"Sometimes, I'm afraid she does." Sadie nibbled a crust she'd "accidentally" broken off. "She was captain of the cheerleading squad during high school, and she still keeps several of those outfits in her closet for this time of year. She wears them every day, right through the end of the tourney. Even to church if we win the sectional."

Liz opened her mouth to ask what a sectional was, but Mary Ann entered, looking as brisk and together as always, despite her odd getup. Liz swallowed her questions and steered them toward the table. *Let's start with pie. Everything looks better post-pie.*

She directed their conversation toward the new grandchild of fellow Material Girl Opal Ringenberg.

"The first girl in her family," Sadie crowed. "All those dark curls. She's the spitting image of her daddy."

"Let's make little Madison Ruby a ruffly pillow to match the quilt we sewed," Mary Ann cooed. "I'll cut out the pieces tonight."

Mellowed by baby chatter and second helpings of pie, it seemed the two might be ready to discuss their conflict sans owl throwing. Liz ventured, "Can I help you with the decorations?"

Both froze, forks in midair.

"You can help me burn them." Sadie pointed her fork at Mary Ann.

Liz sighed. *Yeah, you're the sane one.*

Mary Ann swallowed. "I do not understand your attitude. We are shop owners. In order to sell, we meet the needs—and tastes—of our customers. Of our community."

Sadie sniffed. "The Amish never go to basketball games."

"But the rest of Pleasant Creek has for generations. Everyone but you." Mary Ann tsk-tsked into her coffee. "I cannot understand how a born-and-raised Hoosier can disregard our rich basketball heritage."

"Heritage?" Sadie snorted. "I'm all about preserving our heritage. I'm the one who takes pictures of every event, remember? Every parade, every spelling contest, every baby tooth breaking through. I just won't participate in something as stupid as Hoosier Hysteria."

"We cannot afford to ignore the interests of our clientele." Mary Ann matched Sadie's posture. "Therefore, I *will* decorate our shop with the team colors in support of our community." Her words formed a barrier as delicate and unyielding as wrought iron.

Liz hazarded a suggestion: "Perhaps we could reach some middle ground here?"

"I shall," Sadie said, imitating Mary Ann's high-and-mighty manner, "if I can get a word in edgewise."

"Please do." Mary Ann sipped her coffee, pinkie upraised.

"I agree to ignore the cheerleading outfit—"

"Really?" Shocked out of her proper English tea persona, Mary Ann leveled a suspicious look at her friend.

"Really. But please don't do cheers at work this year." Sadie raised her chin. "It's embarrassing."

This from a woman who wore umbrella-size, neon-flowered hats and had been known to tango through the inn with a rose between her teeth.

Liz prayed silently. And reached for a third piece of pie.

"All right." Mary Ann leaned across the table until they were almost nose to nose. "I will accede to your request—if you will not make a fuss about my decorating *my* shop."

"You can decorate *part* of *my* shop," Sadie countered as she served herself more coffee. "Set up your basketball shrine in the back—"

"The front." Now Mary Ann stuck out her chin. "You will not obscure our town's heritage just because of your prejudices."

"All right, all right, the front." Sadie slammed down her mug and raked her fingers through her short, gray hair. "But only in the fabric area. I'm sick and tired of banging my head into owls swinging from the ceiling whenever I help someone find a pattern."

Liz knew she should keep quiet, but she couldn't resist asking, "Um, could someone explain the owls?"

"Why, that's our team's mascot." Mary Ann stared at her as if she'd questioned gravity. "The Mighty Owls. Would you like to hear our school song?" She stood and snapped to attention as if about to salute.

"No, no! I can't take it this early. And no school song will be played in our shop. Ever. Nor videos," Sadie decreed. "Not even one."

Thankfully, vigorous debate diverted Mary Ann from a demonstration of the school song and, Liz suspected, the routine that went with it. With each bite of pie, the opponents' volume dropped a little. When the ceramic pie plate held only a few crumbs, Liz nudged the two toward their shop. Despite her bloated stomach's protests, she raced to her apartment as soon as they left the kitchen.

Safe at last. Liz turned the dead bolt, panting as if she'd run a marathon. She set the alarm on her phone and fell into bed, hoping for a few minutes of rest before starting on the busy day's to-do list.

Just as Liz dozed off, a raucous cheer assaulted the quiet. Mary Ann belted out the words over Sadie's protests:

> *We are the Mighty Owls!*
> *On field or court, we're not your pals.*
> *The orange and black, with beak and claws*
> *Will win the victory because*
> *We are the Mighty Owls!*
> *Swooping down with mighty howls . . .*

Liz moaned. March Madness? She wasn't sure she'd live through February.

2

"Less than three weeks left until the first sectional game," Ruth Bontrager told Mary Ann as they rocked in Sew Welcome's spacious workroom, embroidering squares for the tournament quilt. Ruth, the fiftyish, fuzzy-haired president of the Pleasant Creek Basketball Booster Club, wasn't a member of the Material Girls, the quilting group that met at Sew Welcome each week. But she apparently helped make the tournament quilt every year.

In the off-season, Ruth consistently wore faded denim jumpers. Today, though, her cheerleader outfit out-oranged Mary Ann's. The two yakked about the latest high school basketball polls while they and the other Material Girls—Liz, Sadie, Caitlyn Ross, and Opal Ringenberg—cut, sewed, and pressed.

Despite her participation in the activity, Sadie shot an evil look at Ruth and Mary Ann, obviously annoyed by all of their basketball chatter.

Great. Ruth's a red-haired version of Mary Ann. Fresh from spending an expensive few minutes with a refrigerator repairman, Liz held her breath. But Sadie had evidently elected to play nice today. Liz tried not to *whoosh* a sigh of relief as her basketball-hating friend turned away and focused on the quilt.

Liz grabbed squares to baste. "I know we're raffling off this quilt to benefit the basketball program, but I have no idea what it's going to look like."

"Mary Ann and I designed it," Ruth said proudly as she pulled a drawing from a folder.

From the corner of her eye, Liz noticed a small scowl Sadie couldn't hide. More was going on here than basketball. Perhaps a little jealousy?

"It's a scoreboard, see? With Pleasant Creek scoring a hundred and visitors scoring thirteen. For bad luck." Ruth beamed. "There won't be another quilt like it anywhere."

Liz could believe that. The tournament quilt, done in the school colors, plus touches of bright yellow and blue, would have looked garish but for the artistry of its creators. Yes, she could see supporters handing over big bucks for the privilege of showing off their team loyalty to other envious fans.

Ruth put away the drawing. "It'll be even better than the one we made in '02, when we went to the state semifinals." Wistfulness crossed her chubby face, quickly eclipsed by a wave of anger. "We might have made finals this year, even won state, if only Asher Hilty hadn't gotten himself thrown off the team. You'd think an Amish boy would know how to behave himself."

Prim, seventyish Opal moved from the cutting table to pat her shoulder. "Now, Ruthie—"

"You know it's true." The booster club president's face flamed to match her hair. "Asher left the Amish community and weaseled his way into free room and board at Coach's house. Coach made him a basketball star. But was that kid grateful? No, he had to ruin everything for everyone!"

Silence.

Liz glanced from face to face. What had this troubled teen done to cause such a hush?

"Asher hasn't ruined anything," Mary Ann said pleasantly, as if Ruth were still smiling. "Our boys will play hard with or without him. And I think this quilt *will* top the one from '02."

Ruth's face flushed a deeper red, and her voice quieted. "You're right. Our team will do their best. And the proceeds from this year's quilt will help buy the equipment they need."

Opal mentioned a spaghetti supper and other fund-raisers, and soon Ruth was cheerfully gabbing about presectional game events—and selling tickets.

"Don't miss Ruth's banner this Saturday," Mary Ann urged Liz. "She makes a new one every year for the Banner Buzz."

Liz assumed this was another tournament-time ritual. "Do they, uh . . . hang it in the gym?"

"Oh no." Mary Ann knotted a new strand of floss. "The best place to see it is behind Opal's barn."

"I'll save you a spot, Liz," Opal called from her cutting table.

Save me a spot? To see a banner behind a barn? Liz poked her needle through the cloth a little harder than necessary. *No. I won't ask.*

Mary Ann glanced at her. "Don't worry, dear. Ruth never buzzes too close. She's very conscientious about safety."

"She is," Caitlyn said, and the other guests nodded.

From the ironing board, Sadie flung at Mary Ann, "There was the time that poor man had to go to the emergency room."

"Ruth had nothing to do with that," Mary Ann retorted.

"He shouldn't have been there." Ruth's brown eyes snapped. "His pacemaker battery was low."

Liz could stand it no more. "What are you talking about?"

As if on cue, all the quilters paused. Their eyes widened like those of calves in a field.

Then Opal chuckled. "I suppose if you haven't attended one of Ruth's Banner Buzzes, none of this makes sense. Ruth's a pilot."

Liz stared at Ruth. "I thought you were a pharmacist. That you owned a drugstore."

"I do. My family's owned it for a hundred years. But I've flown since I was a teenager and got my license when I turned eighteen." She pulled out her phone and showed Liz a black-and-white photo of a freckle-faced girl grinning in front of a small plane. "Used to do crop dusting. Now I mostly fly for fun."

"And, boy, is her banner buzzing fun," Caitlyn chimed in. "She flies the Orange Rules banner all over the county—"

"So Delemont and Blaketown can see it." Mary Ann chuckled nastily. "And Bergen and Stoneville and Wildton."

"We have to make sure those folks know we'll win," Ruth declared.

"She does loop-de-loops too. But she flies extra low over *our* fields." Opal looked excited.

Mary Ann laughed. "Some of the townspeople dress up as opposing basketball players and mascots. She chases them all over the fields."

"Everybody comes to the Banner Buzz," Caitlyn enthused, "even some of the Amish boys—the ones who are still at the *Rumschpringe* stage."

At least Liz knew what that meant. Only unbaptized Amish teens, still free to explore "English" ways, would attend an event like that. What did her Amish relations think of this bizarre basketball scenario?

The bells that announced Sew Welcome's customers normally rang a sweet welcome. But now, a slam and harsh jangle interrupted Liz's thoughts.

The startled quilters raised their heads. Both Mary Ann and Sadie rushed to the workroom's entrance.

Their visitor burst in before they could reach the door. "Is Naomi here?" Kate Linder demanded in a choked voice.

Liz had met Kate, a high school phys ed teacher, through Naomi Mason, a fellow Material Girl and good friend. Though initially reserved, Kate smiled more lately, especially when she was eating doughnuts with Coach John Albertson at Naomi's bakery.

"No, her dad had to go to the hospital. She left early for Indianapolis." Mary Ann put her hands on the woman's shoulders. "What's wrong, dear? Can we help you?"

Liz cringed at the sight of Kate's empty eyes. *Like sockets in a skull.*

"Nobody can help me." The woman spoke in a parched monotone. "John died today."

3

Coach Albertson is dead? Liz stared in surprise.

"How?" For once, Ruth's brassy tone dwindled to a whisper. "Car accident? Heart attack?"

"Don't know. No accident." Each word seemed to cost Kate a limb.

Mary Ann, shaking off her own shock, encircled the teacher with a hug. "Let Dr. Sam determine that. Right now, you need to think of you."

Liz helped Kate to the library, then raced to the kitchen, where she found Sadie already brewing tea for the distraught woman.

Liz loaded a tray with refreshments for the quilters, which Sadie carried to Sew Welcome. Then Liz took the tea to the library. When Kate didn't reach for the mug or even look up, Liz placed it on an end table next to the sofa. She sat in a chair opposite.

Mary Ann coaxed, "Perhaps it would do you good to talk about it."

"Good? I doubt it." A small sign of life stirred Kate's blank face with this denial.

"Did they take John to the hospital?" Mary Ann handed Kate the tea.

"No. No hospital." Her colorless lips barely moved. "I . . . found him this afternoon. At his office. He was . . . already gone."

Today was Monday, when the school was bursting with activity. Had no one noticed the man's death before then? Questions flew to Liz's lips, but she kept quiet. This poor woman didn't need an interrogation.

"At first, I thought he'd fallen asleep at his desk," Kate continued in the same toneless voice. "But his eyes were open. His face . . ." Her own face crumpled, and she covered it with her hands. Her shoulders shook, yet she didn't make a sound.

Mary Ann gently rubbed her back.

Feeling like an intruder, Liz gestured toward the door.

Mary Ann nodded and mouthed, "I'll take Kate home."

Liz slipped back to Sew Welcome, already hearing the relentless hum of questions rising over Pleasant Creek like a storm cloud. When she entered, the quilters had circled their chairs, hands strangely idle.

"I can't believe he's gone." Caitlyn dabbed at her eyes. "John Albertson has coached here a long time."

"At least twenty-five years." The bad news had not cracked Opal's composure, but her mouth trembled a little. "Coach's ex-wife, Natalie, used to belong to a sorority that did projects with mine. Even when she moved to Indianapolis after the divorce, we kept in touch until she passed away from cancer."

"Coach was a pain in the you-know-what sometimes, but I can't picture the team without him." Ruth kept her tone steady, but moist eyes betrayed her emotion. "The boys will be devastated. Absolutely devastated."

Apparently, Ruth saw the entire world through an "our team" filter. But she was right. The players would be devastated, as would the whole high school and all of Pleasant Creek.

Sadie scanned Liz's face. "Did Kate say how it happened?"

"Only that she found him in his office this afternoon." Soon the entire town would know that much, so Liz didn't feel she was betraying a confidence.

"Oh, my." Opal clucked her tongue. "No one was at school today. How terrible. If he'd gotten sick any other day, someone would have called 911."

"But it's a Monday," Liz protested, "and not a holiday. Why wasn't anyone else there?"

"My daughter told me the high school would be closed today. She and all the other teachers were attending a training session at Blaketown," Opal explained. "Only the central office was open, and it's on the other side of the school."

"Why didn't Coach go to Blaketown too? Isn't he a teacher?"

"Oh no. He's never taught classes, though he practically lives at the school," Caitlyn said. "He doubles as athletic director and basketball coach." She bit her lip. "Or doubled, I guess."

Sadie glanced around the circle. "Maybe we should call it quits for today."

Liz nodded with the others. At this point, did they know if the sectional games would even be played?

She thought briefly of the alumni who'd already made reservations at the inn for the next few weekends and how much the town must depend on this midwinter burst of tourism. Liz's optimistic outlook for her inn faded with Opal's and Caitlyn's retreating footsteps.

What's the matter with me? A man has died. Still, she could not erase the bill for a new refrigerator from her mind. Losing guests who might come for the games and festivities would destroy the profit cushion she'd imagined for this winter.

Sadie sighed. "You going back to the drugstore, Ruth?"

"Maybe. I don't feel like doing anything right now." Glumly, Ruth gathered her work into a tote. "Tomorrow I'll talk with the principal about what'll be cancelled and what sort of memorial there will be. Coach's death is a terrible blow to everything. Terrible."

Uncharacteristically quiet, Sadie folded fabric and gathered notions. Her eyes misted as she cleared the workroom with Liz. Despite her scorn for Hoosier Hysteria, Sadie wasn't cheering.

Maybe no one would for quite a while.

———— *//////////////////////////* ————

"If you receive calls for me, would you take messages and slip them under my door?" Corinne Albertson spoke so low Liz could hardly hear her.

"Of course." Standing behind the inn's desk, Liz handed the woman in her late twenties a pen to sign the registry. Liz had almost dropped her phone when Coach's daughter called late the previous day to reserve a room. Why would she stay here instead of her dad's home? Or in a nearby town if she wanted privacy?

Now, watching Corinne sign her name using tiny, careful script, Liz recited the usual breakfast and coffee-hour information.

Corinne smoothed her dark chignon. "I . . . may not eat breakfast. Coffee and cookies would be nice, but . . ."

"I'll bring some to your room." Liz had to restrain herself from patting the trim woman's suited shoulder. "Breakfast too, if you like. We'll do everything we can to ensure your privacy."

"Thank you." Corinne's expression didn't change. She insisted on carrying her sleek luggage herself.

Liz watched her climb the stairs. She knew that orphan feeling. Liz's dad had died when she was a preschooler, and she'd lost her mother last year.

One orphan couldn't help but share another's pain.

———— *//////////////////////////* ————

"I wish everyone would stop whispering whenever Kate goes anywhere." Naomi Mason gestured toward the front window of her bakery, Sweet Everything.

"She looks terrible." Liz sipped her coffee and watched Kate struggle to open the glass door. Had Kate slept an hour since John's death? Then Liz realized—too late—that she'd lowered her voice. "We're whispering too."

Naomi thumped the table, rattling her own mug. "Blast," she muttered. Recovering her usual smile, she waved Kate across the near-empty bakery to their booth. "Liz and I need someone to be lazy with us."

"Yeah, lazy." Liz copied Naomi's light tone. *Right.* Naomi usually rose before four in the morning to get started on her baked goods.

Naomi patted the seat beside her. "Want a snack?"

"No." For a moment, Kate took a step away, as if she wanted to run. But her shoulders slumped, and she dropped into the booth beside Naomi.

"I'll get coffee." Liz scooted from her place. "Decaf or the real stuff, Kate? Hazelnut, mocha, vanilla?"

"Real. Black, no flavoring. Naomi's brew."

Sweet Everything's customers knew that every midafternoon the owner brewed a couple of pots of dark roast, guaranteed to help the drowsiest worker stay energized until five.

Liz went to the coffee bar and brought back a steaming mug for Kate.

Naomi slipped an arm around Kate, who drooped into her embrace. No one said anything. Finally, Kate raised her head. "Thanks for not asking how I feel."

People were only trying to show their concern, Liz knew. Yet a bereaved person might feel as if a hundred reporters were thrusting microphones into her face, yelling, "What was your reaction when you realized the person you loved more than life was gone forever?"

"I just came from the funeral home." Kate's voice shook. "Tom Yoder was kind, but, bottom line, I have no say in John's . . . funeral."

Naomi gently rubbed her shoulders. Liz exchanged helpless glances with her fellow Material Girl. She didn't know Kate or John well. Should she leave and let Naomi try to ease this poor woman's pain? She pointed toward herself and then the door.

Naomi shook her head slightly.

Okay, friend. Maybe she could help out if Naomi had customers.

Suddenly Kate straightened. "All the decisions are to be made by his daughter. They haven't spoken in years, but that doesn't matter." She glared at the pretty coral-and-gray place mats on the table, then raised her gaze to Naomi's sympathetic doe eyes. "After basketball season, John and I planned to shop for rings. He'd already persuaded me to move our wedding up to June and was trying to talk me into eloping during spring break." Tears boiled down her cheeks. "Yet I'm not even allowed to see him until *she* says I can."

Corinne's immovable face floated through Liz's mind. Maybe grief had hardened her attractive features into that white-marble mask. Liz hoped her heart had not followed suit.

Naomi ventured, "Perhaps if you ask . . ."

"I did," Kate snapped. Then with a stricken look, she said, "I'm sorry. It's just that I've heard nothing. Tom said he asked her if I could spend a half hour in private with him—his . . . body. But she hasn't given an answer. It's like I don't exist. Like nothing *I* feel matters." Her head and shoulders shrank into a silent, shuddering ball.

Naomi murmured comforting words.

Liz prayed for Kate. *Lord, please help her. Help us.*

Kate's spasm quieted. But when she spoke again, her flat tone made Liz's skin crawl. "But that's not even the worst of all this. I believe John was murdered."

Naomi's eyes widened.

Liz stuttered, "M-murdered? Did Dr. Sam—?"

"Of course, he examined John. He's the county coroner as well as a family doctor. Sam told the police he died of a heart attack." She glowered at Liz as if she were responsible for her misery. Kate lowered her voice and hissed, "But I think John was poisoned."

Realizing she was shaking her head, Liz froze.

Naomi's reasonable voice broke the awful silence. "John was over fifty, wasn't he? And he didn't take care of himself very well."

Everyone knew Coach considered Naomi's bakery his home away from home, second only to his office. And John Albertson hadn't come for the company; he'd always ignored Naomi when she'd tried to steer him toward the bran muffins.

"He'd been doing better since we started dating in November," Kate protested, thrusting her words like daggers. "You know he received those emails at the season's start—the ones that threatened to get him fired."

Naomi nodded. "Well, there are always a few fans who get carried away."

Especially when a team has several losing seasons in a row. Though Liz had largely ignored basketball until recently, she couldn't help but hear rumblings against Coach Albertson after practices started last fall.

"Things got better when he recruited Asher. John believed he would help them win state for the first time in Pleasant Creek's history. We thought the losing streak would be over." Kate collapsed into tears again and couldn't speak.

Liz had heard of Asher's accident, which had occurred soon after Christmas, but Naomi filled in the details now. Driving an Amish friend's buggy after a few drinks, Asher ran a stop sign. A pickup struck the buggy, injuring Asher's friend and killing the horse. Asher had been arrested on the spot.

"Asher did that after John let him live with him. Provided him with clothes and books. Opened a chance for him to go to college on scholarship. Perhaps even play professionally. You'd think that kid would show some gratitude. Or at least behave like he had a brain." Kate raised a shaky hand to her forehead. "Instead, Asher threw everything away for a buggy joyride. He went to jail for a month. John had no choice but to dismiss him from the team a week after Christmas. Yet Asher blames John for all his troubles.

"Even before this, they fought constantly. In November John thought Asher might have keyed his truck—scratched the finish all the way around. That same night, Asher probably spray-painted graffiti on my garage to get back at him. After John kicked Asher off the team somebody slashed John's tires." Kate stabbed the air with a finger. "It's not that hard to figure out who."

She bit her trembling lip. "John told me Asher got out of jail a week or two ago. I know he crashed on John's couch at least once. He's a very smart kid, and he's learned how to search the Internet. He could find out about poisons."

Enough to fool Sam Schneider? Liz, still a newcomer, didn't know the doctor well, but he had a reputation as a caring and conscientious physician.

Naomi's mouth crinkled sideways in what Liz had learned was her doubtful expression. But she only said, "Are you taking care of yourself? I can warm up a bowl of homemade vegetable soup. You shouldn't be alone right now—"

"But I am alone." Kate's desolate gaze tore at Liz's heart. "John loved me, and I wasn't alone anymore. Now someone's taken him away from me. I have no one."

"You have friends," Naomi said firmly. She gave Kate a little push. "Let me out. I'll bring you the soup, then you can rest on the cot I use when I've got a lot of dough rising during the night."

After Naomi bustled off, Kate dropped into the booth again, her wavy, sandy hair hanging in her heart-shaped face and her chin pressed into her lacy top. She looked like an abandoned rag doll. Liz longed to pick her up and hug her.

Instead, she sat beside the bereaved woman and held her cold hand, saying little. When customers entered and Naomi waited on them, Liz remained with Kate while she ate half a bowl of the hot, fragrant soup and nibbled on a fresh-baked roll. Kate didn't fight Naomi's insistence that she rest in the back room. She closed her eyes almost before she lay down.

Naomi shut the door and walked Liz to the front entrance. She glanced at the two customers eating doughnuts in a back booth and whispered, "I hope a little food and sleep will help dispel this idea that someone poisoned John."

"So do I. That man was a heart attack waiting to happen," Liz murmured. "You're right. She shouldn't be alone. Does she have any relatives?"

"A dad in Michigan who'd be more trouble than help. A few cousins on the West Coast." Naomi clucked her tongue regretfully.

Picturing Kate and Corinne in the same house, Liz said, "I'd invite Kate to stay with me a day or two, but I'm afraid that wouldn't be a good idea."

Naomi grimaced. "You're right about that."

Glancing at the booth where Liz had last seen Kate with Coach, Liz recalled how her pale, slightly freckled face had glowed as the big, loud man teased her. She'd even thrown out a taunt or two herself, pink lips curving in a saucy smile.

Liz, mostly content with her singleness, had wondered then what on earth Kate saw in John Albertson. He wore wrinkled, outdated shirts that barely contained his bulging belly. A bad haircut made the cowlicks in his thick gray hair worse. He inevitably said what he thought—not always a good quality in a coach or a boyfriend. But Kate had loved him, and Liz had seen the way he looked at her, like she was the only woman in the world.

Now he was gone.

Liz understood Kate's shock and denial, her need to blame someone. But to say it was murder? That seemed like a huge long shot.

A delusion that would only hurt Kate more.

4

We *should have been cheering at the basketball game tonight*, Liz thought, watching cars pull into the high school parking lot as she prepared to help distribute candles to those who had braved the cold to attend a vigil for Coach Albertson.

"Everybody gets one, but give candles for the younger kids to their parents," Sadie instructed. "We don't want them setting each other on fire."

Good idea. Pleasant Creek needed no more grief. As Liz handed candles to stunned attendees, she marveled how Mary Ann and Ruth, though mourning too, quietly took care of the details and comforted others. Sadie, who had photographed each and every town event for decades and served along with Mary Ann as Pleasant Creek's unofficial historians, readied a large video camera to film the event.

Corinne's stoic countenance popped into Liz's mind, as it often had throughout the day. Coach's daughter had hardly changed expressions since she'd arrived. Would she show more emotion at this vigil?

More than two hundred townspeople gathered in the chilly twilight to honor Coach Albertson, but Corinne did not appear.

You should be here, Liz told her silently.

Corinne had lived here as a child, gone to school in Pleasant Creek. Didn't old friends enter into her picture at all? *Why haven't you come?*

In contrast, Kate, a pale wraith, stood shivering between Naomi and Mary Ann at the head of the mourners. Liz feared Kate would collapse before Pastor Brad of Pleasant Creek Community Church finished his brief devotional.

Liz knew that Kate had communicated with Corinne through Tom Yoder, the funeral director. John Albertson's daughter must be aware of the relationship.

Had Kate's presence kept Corinne from this gathering? Liz glanced at the parking lot closest to the school's back entrances. Perhaps Corinne had seen Kate and left?

At the end of the vigil, Robert Oaks, the high school principal, announced that the game scheduled for Thursday would also be cancelled, as well as the presectional festivities until Monday, when the Day of the Draw would be held as usual. The other sectional events and games would take place after that, just as Coach Albertson would have wanted.

A relieved murmur met his words, and the crowd dispersed.

Later, as they sat with other somber mourners at Sweet Everything, Mary Ann commented on Corinne's absence. "I wasn't really surprised. Coach spent very little time with his family, which was why Natalie divorced him. Corinne probably hadn't spoken with him in years."

If Mary Ann didn't know something about each and every family in Pleasant Creek, it wasn't worth knowing. So Kate was right about the Albertsons' estrangement. But that certainly didn't validate her insistence that Coach had been poisoned.

The next day, Liz stood in a long line snaking out the funeral home doors and down the block.

"Why didn't she have the funeral at the gym?" groused Sadie, standing with Liz and the other Material Girls. "That's what Jim Haroldson's family did—you know, the principal back in the seventies—when he died of a heart attack. Then we wouldn't have to stand in the cold."

"At least it's a beautiful day." Liz rewrapped her scarf around her throat. "No sleet."

Apprehension pricked Liz's thoughts. What if Corinne didn't show up here either? Or worse, what if both she and Kate did?

The Material Girls stepped onto Yoder's large front porch, where Ruth, bundled to her eyebrows, sat at a small table. The booster club president dabbed at her wet eyes with a tissue. "Remember Coach Albertson with a gift to his team" read the placard beside her. It was discreet, thank goodness. No big, gaudy banners. Still, Liz found it a little out of place at the funeral home.

Yet Ruth's appeal for booster club funds apparently resonated with the mourners; many stopped to write checks or stuff a few bills into the donation box.

Finally, Liz and the other Material Girls entered the venerable front door and paused by a sizable display of photos, trophies, and other mementos in the foyer. Coach Albertson had played basketball at Pleasant Creek and Indiana State University, then returned to his alma mater as an assistant coach, eventually taking over the head position. Despite the cowlicks that had plagued him even then, he had been a handsome young man and an imposing player. For the first time, Liz noticed that Corinne's eyes and facial structure resembled his, cast in a feminine mold.

"How did Corinne dig up all these pictures?" she whispered to Sadie.

"She didn't. Ruth asked me to help her find them. We spent most of last night here, setting this up."

Sadie set up a basketball display? Liz's initial disbelief quickly faded. Of course, Sadie would not let her distaste for basketball interfere with serving her community and easing its grief.

Moving past the display, the Material Girls entered the funeral home's main room. Tom Yoder had not yet replaced the splashy cranberry, green, and mauve carpet that Mary Ann abhorred. "He'd better do something about that before my last party," she'd told Liz, "or I'll come back to haunt him."

The small smile Liz gleaned from their past banter didn't soothe her growing uneasiness. She spotted Corinne at the far end of the room by the casket. She wore her signature nonexpression, set in cold white stone. Grief? Rage? Both?

Where was Kate? Liz searched the room row by row without seeing the grieving teacher. Had she decided to stay away?

As they neared the front, Liz's gaze shifted to the casket. Dressed in a navy suit and tasteful tie, the coach looked better than she'd ever seen him. Someone had given him probably the best haircut of his life. Liz assumed Corinne had seen to these details. Had she bought the suit? Or had Coach purchased it himself . . . perhaps for his wedding?

Sudden tears filled Liz's eyes. She wiped them away in time to see Corinne's eyes illuminate for the first time. But not with warmth. Their laser-like rays stabbed the sandy-haired woman standing before her.

Kate.

Mary Ann slipped toward the front, but Naomi, standing behind Kate, had already edged between Kate and Corinne. Wearing a subdued version of her usual infectious smile, Naomi introduced them as if both women had stopped in at her bakery for cream puffs. Then Naomi steered Kate to a small niche by the head of the casket while Mary Ann caught Corinne's attention with a heartfelt yet wordy tribute to her father. Liz choked when Sadie joined in the near eulogy.

While the two talked to Corinne, Kate focused on Coach's uncharacteristically serene face. She touched his cheek with one finger, then gently kissed his lips.

A soft murmur filtered through the crowd.

Corinne whirled around, but Kate had already turned away, Naomi guiding her to a seat near the front. Mary Ann and Sadie disappeared into one of the last rows.

When Liz, Opal, and Caitlyn expressed their sympathies to Corinne, her eyes still shot silver flashes of anger, and a smear of red like a rash erupted on her pale face. However, when Liz offered her hand, Corinne grasped it like a drowning swimmer, and her taut mouth eased slightly. Liz realized that no relatives or old friends stood beside Corinne in front of her father's coffin. *Am I one of the few people here she knows? Surely not. She used to live in this town.*

Liz sat next to strangers because the chairs had filled quickly. The reserved rows were taken by grief-stricken teen boys wearing various odd versions of ill-fitting dress clothes—the basketball team, no doubt.

Several red-eyed girls in cheerleader outfits joined them. All wore black armbands.

She noticed that Corinne appeared to recognize a few of the visitors, including Ruth, who had finally abandoned her booster club table. Liz's angst relaxed a bit when Principal Oaks hugged Corinne and a few retired teachers greeted her warmly. Then Pastor Brad spoke to her and escorted her to a front seat.

As the minister returned to the podium, a stir arose in the back, growing every second.

Liz tried to maintain propriety, but she turned slightly, just as a tall boy with blue-streaked blond hair ambled past her down the aisle.

"Asher . . . Asher . . ." The whispered name rustled through the crowd like leaves before a storm.

Asher Hilty. The Amish player Coach had nurtured, then kicked off the team.

The teen's rocker hair and good looks contrasted strangely with his Amish black pants and white shirt. For a second Liz's eyes locked with Asher's. His blue eyes, the color of cyanide, were unblinking . . . haunted . . .

Guilty?

5

Kate had all but accused Asher of killing his coach that day at Naomi's, but Liz hadn't even considered the possibility, focused mostly on the idea that in her grief, Kate was searching for someone to blame. But seeing the boy now gave Liz pause. Did Asher, furious about his dismissal, find a way to take revenge on the man who had encouraged, then destroyed his basketball career?

But the kid was Amish and obviously still affected by his background. Surely the Amish stance against violence continued to resonate within him.

Asher was only a few years younger than Steve, Liz's godson whom she had raised. She winced, remembering their shouting matches during his teens after he'd done something stupid. She'd always been terrified that Steve would do something worse—make a mistake he couldn't get past. Had Asher, newly freed from the constraints of an Amish upbringing, done that something worse? But how could he? Why would he? What if a heated confrontation with Albertson had triggered a heart attack? That was possible. Teenagers could say some horrible things. Or what if Asher had done something more calculated?

Liz's thoughts bombarded her, making it difficult to concentrate on the minister's short sermon. Though the room quieted after Asher sat with the team, she knew the rest of the congregation struggled to listen as well. *Poor Pastor Brad.* He was trying to comfort a polite audience who heard nothing.

Liz forced her attention back to the pastor as he talked about John Albertson's loyalty to his players and his commitment to excellence on the basketball court. The pastor spoke of his flaws, even eliciting a few chuckles as he referred to Coach's doughnut addiction.

Now he was speaking of the man's new, imperfect faith in Christ. "John told me he regretted much of his past. 'Not doing so great now, Pastor,' he said. 'Still losing more than winning.' But his heart had changed."

Liz hadn't heard that part of Coach's story, though she had recently seen him with Kate at Pleasant Creek Community Church. How sad that he had not lived long enough to share his life of faith with Kate.

Once Pastor Brad finished and Tom Yoder started dismissing rows of people, Liz wondered about Asher again. Given the emotional situation, she certainly expected him to be upset. Asher walked past her, gaze fixed on his feet, hunched as if something inside him had shriveled.

The big room emptied slowly as the mourners returned to their cars. Liz, driving behind Sadie's incongruous hot pink Jeep, saw that townspeople lined the route to the cemetery, hats removed on this cold day. Whatever they had thought of his coaching style, Pleasant Creek citizens remembered their own.

After parking near the cemetery, Liz walked toward the canopy that was set up over the coach's grave. She glanced at the crowd but didn't see Asher with the team. She joined the other Material Girls standing behind the few rows of chairs under the tent.

Liz had feared a scene between Kate and Corinne, but the women sat at opposite ends of the first row, ignoring each other. Kate rose almost immediately after the pastor's brief words.

Naomi and the other Material Girls walked her to Naomi's car. Seeing Kate surrounded by friends, Liz murmured her sympathy to the weary, pallid woman again, excused herself, and went back to the grave.

The few remaining attendees clustered a short distance from the tent, and Corinne sat inside alone. She leveled a blank look at Liz, then turned away.

Liz stood nearby, saying nothing. When Corinne walked to her sleek sedan, Liz followed. "Would you like me to drive you to the inn? We can arrange to pick up your car later. Or I can take you to get something to eat." She doubted Corinne wanted to attend the community potluck Ruth and Mary Ann had planned.

Corinne did not face her. "No . . . but thank you. Thank you very much."

Liz watched her drive away, wishing she knew what else to do.

"Can I help you find something?" Loretta Simmons asked.

Liz looked up from a pile of newspapers and returned the Pleasant Creek librarian's friendly smile. "No, thanks. I've found most of what I need already."

Um, not quite *true.* Still, Liz breathed a sigh of relief as Loretta returned to shelving books in the biography section.

Loretta probably could have located the information Liz wanted with a snap of her fingers. But she'd also try—nicely, of course—to extract why Liz wanted to know about the vandalism that had plagued Pleasant Creek the past several months. And for a librarian, Loretta certainly liked to talk.

Liz could have investigated the incidents at the courthouse, but she had delved into their trove of public records last spring when she was investigating a human bone Beans had dug up in an unusual display of energy. Neither the town nor Kate needed to know about Liz's examination of those vandalism incidents—unless something significant turned up.

If only the newspapers or local records were digitized. With a few clicks, she could have accomplished her search in privacy. Instead, she dug through pages and pages of stories about tractor shows, PTA meetings, and euchre tournaments.

Liz found herself reading a couple of articles that featured Jackson Cross. Such a proactive mayor, always looking out for Pleasant Creek.

The newspaper pictures of him didn't do him justice. Closing her eyes, Liz pictured fortyish Jackson, his twinkling hazel eyes, rugged good looks, and grin that melted the heart of every woman in town . . .

But not hers. At least not right now. The two of them had grown closer during the holiday season when Jackson had helped her unmask a person bent on revenge. He'd also taken Liz to the Christmas parade. But then Steve had unexpectedly come home on leave, and she'd spent every minute she could with her godson before he had to return to Kosovo.

By then Jackson was running a busy post-holiday sale at his handcrafted furniture store. After that, he'd done inventory and begun hectic preparations for a spring show.

Lately, they hadn't seen each other much.

Did she want to see Jackson more? Liz twisted a lock of her hair. She liked him. A lot. But having recently tangled with Matt, her ex-boyfriend, she preferred to take it slow and easy with Jackson—*if* he wanted to see *her*. Which he might not. Did he?

Stop acting like a teenager with a crush. Flushing, Liz opened a different newspaper. *Focus. I need to find some hard facts about the vandalism.*

Liz reviewed incidents from September through January. The number increased around Halloween with most cases involving the destruction of mailboxes and the tipping of outhouses, particularly in Amish areas. Vandalism then decreased with cold weather—until Liz pinpointed when Coach Albertson had dismissed Asher from the basketball team: the week after Christmas. Coach's yard had been TPed twice. Kate hadn't mentioned that, but throwing toilet paper in a high school teacher's trees was hardly out of the ordinary. Somebody had tossed garbage onto his back porch. Another trickster had left a dead raccoon on his front doorstep. Finally, toward the end of that week, his tires had been slashed, one incident Kate *had* related.

But where were the other incidents Kate had mentioned? Liz didn't expect to find newspaper accounts of the threatening emails Coach had received. He and the police probably kept those quiet. But surely the keying of Coach's truck and the spray-painting of Kate's garage would have made the local paper. Liz leafed back through several weeks.

There it was in a late November edition. She skimmed the lines of the brief account. It matched Kate's description of the two incidents but without naming a suspect. Liz also noted pictures of a basketball game in which Pleasant Creek, with Asher's assistance, had continued its incredible dominance.

That vandalism had taken place when the basketball team was rolling over every opponent. At that point, fans were counting on playing in the state tournament. Had it been an election year, Coach Albertson could have run for office and won. No one would have attacked him then—nor would anyone have wanted to hear anything bad about Asher.

Liz rubbed her forehead. What had precipitated that isolated double incident? Coach Albertson and his star player had been known to disagree. Had he and Asher clashed in a particularly nasty argument? One so bad that Asher harassed Coach's girlfriend, as well as keyed his truck?

Most teen boys Liz had known might have fit a TP/garbage/dead-raccoon profile. But she didn't know Asher. Perhaps he was more troubled than everyone realized.

Everyone except Kate.

———— *///////////////////////////* ————

The next day, walking a high school hallway to Coach's office with Kate and Naomi, Liz hoped they could complete their errand quickly, without complications. The cold she'd caught at the funeral yesterday was trying to get her down. Fortunately, Dr. Sam had a cancellation this afternoon, and Liz couldn't afford to linger here long.

For once, could a simple plan stay simple?

Her misgivings grew at the sight of a stern, gray-haired woman barricading the closed door. At their approach, she stiffened but still greeted Kate courteously.

"Good morning, Arlene." Though the coach's girlfriend was dry-eyed, her voice shook, revealing what this small pilgrimage was costing her. "I'd like to retrieve a photo I took of us on John's birthday, one he kept on his desk."

Small folds gathered between the secretary's eyes, but she made no move to vacate her post. "I'm sorry. His daughter asked that no one be allowed in until she goes through his things."

Can Corinne do that? Statutes about private versus public property popped into Liz's head, but she shook them away; small towns often perpetuated their own interpretations of legality.

Kate drooped as if her bones had melted. Just as quickly, she snapped to, chin up. "I only want a photo of the two of us. Trust me, *she* won't want it."

"I'm so sorry. That's what I was told," Arlene repeated.

As she and Kate sparred, Liz sympathized with both. All Kate wanted was one picture of the love of her life. Yet how many others had put Arlene in a similar bind?

As if to answer, footsteps rustled on the other side of the door.

Kate's eyes sparked twin firestorms. "No one's allowed? Then who's in there now?"

Arlene stammered, "I-I . . ."

Pushing past her, Kate swung the door open.

Ruth, holding an old-fashioned coffeepot, blinked at them, an odd expression on her face. "Oh. Hello, Kate. Hey, everybody."

"Ruth keeps her booster club files in Coach's office," Arlene offered lamely.

"Thought I'd take the old coffeepot home," Ruth murmured. "Just something to remember Coach by."

"No, you don't." Kate grabbed the coffeepot and clutched it to her chest. "If I can't have one lousy picture, no coffeepot for you. If I can't go in, you can't. *No one* will. Do you hear me?"

Gaping at her, Ruth rushed past them and wheeled a dolly stacked with files down the hall.

"She shouldn't take those files either. Corinne said she can't." Kate bared her teeth. "And we all have to do what Corinne says, don't we? *Don't we?*"

The bell rang and students spilled into the hallway, aiming curious glances at their normally reserved teacher who stood in the alcove by Arlene's desk, clutching a coffeepot and shooting daggers from her eyes. Liz and Naomi tried to calm her. What if Principal Oaks, Kate's boss, saw her outburst?

Arlene raised her hand. "You're right. It is important that you go in."

What? Liz watched the tide of Kate's rage ebb to silence.

"You miss him." Arlene's eyes moistened. "So do I. Go in and fetch your picture."

Liz would have preferred to remain outside, but as Kate plunged through the door, Naomi nodded toward the office, indicating they should accompany her. Was she afraid Kate would collapse? Whatever the reason, Liz thought having a couple of witnesses wasn't a bad idea.

Together they filled up the windowless office, cluttered with bushels of papers, sports journals, and clipboards. The coach's obsolete computer swam amid a sea of athletic detritus, plus wrinkled napkins and empty snack wrappers. And, yes—Liz tried not to wrinkle her nose—a definite odor of gym shoes pervaded the place.

Kate inhaled the questionable ambience as if she'd reached nirvana. "I told him a thousand times to use air freshener in here," she said softly as she replaced the coffeepot on its hot plate atop an overstuffed bookcase.

Shifting books and trash, Kate unearthed a small frame. In the photo she and Coach Albertson flashed unspeakably happy smiles.

"Is that the clock tower behind you?" Naomi pointed to Pleasant Creek's distinctive downtown landmark.

"Yes. I took that selfie the fourth day of January. His birthday. The day he proposed." Kate touched the coach's face. "He showed me once that he'd written on the back, *Can't wait till June.*" Her face crumpled.

Liz joined Naomi in wrapping an arm around Kate. She sobbed quietly for a few minutes. Then, clasping the photo, she lifted her chin and stepped out the door. Liz trailed her and Naomi, glad for the tiny healing this visit seemed to have started.

Then all three women froze.

Corinne.

She stood in front of Arlene's desk, arms crossed like swords. Though she kept her voice down, she punched each word senseless: "I asked that no one enter my father's office."

Poor Arlene cringed, but Corinne's gaze sliced into Kate. Ruth, who had sneaked back, stood openmouthed behind the coach's furious daughter.

Liz cringed too. Would Kate explode again?

"I'm sorry, sweetie." Even Ruth's brash manner quailed before Corinne's icy wrath. "I just wanted to get my booster club files out of your way."

"Ruth, no one helped my father more than you did. But this is important to me." Corinne's stare still hadn't budged from Kate. "Arlene, remember that Principal Oaks officially agreed to my request. Lock this door now and do not open it again unless I give permission."

The secretary whipped out a key ring, locked the door, and slunk back to her chair. Ruth hurried away.

Corinne hadn't blinked. Neither had Kate.

"I was just leaving. I took only this picture, one I'd given John. But if you really want it, take it." Kate shoved the photo almost under Corinne's nose.

Her opponent's pale face turned purple. She didn't say a word. Didn't move.

"Good morning, ladies." The high school principal's pleasant voice broke the silence. So Principal Oaks had heard the ruckus. A skinny, bespectacled man stood behind him.

Liz bit her lip as the adversaries faced the principal.

"Perhaps I can be of help." Principal Oaks reached for the office keys, still in Arlene's hand. "Thank you, Arlene." He gave her hand a quick pat, then removed Coach's office key from the ring. The secretary visibly relaxed.

The principal addressed Corinne. "I will keep this key for a week or so. No one will enter without my say. If it's absolutely necessary, I will check with you before allowing someone in. You have your father's key, so you can enter as you please. Correct?"

"Yes. Thank you." Corinne's mouth hardly moved, but her tone held so much venom that Liz's mouth fell open in shock.

"Kate, did you want something from Coach's office?"

Lightning flashed in Corinne's eyes.

A flush spread across Kate's white cheeks, but she kept her tone level. "No. I have what I wanted." She held up the photo.

Principal Oaks hardly glanced at it, but a tinge of compassion colored his eyes. He turned to the man behind him. "Nathan, do you need to retrieve playbooks, records, equipment . . . ?"

"Maybe a few things. Coach hadn't been feeling well the past week, so I'd already been using his stuff."

The principal looked at Corinne. Glowering, she gave a barely perceptible nod, and he unlocked the office, leaving the door wide open. The man Liz assumed was an assistant coach ducked inside and exited within a few minutes, carrying several notebooks. He hurried across the hall into another small office.

"Then I believe we're done here." Principal Oaks still spoke in an affable tone, but it signaled a definite dismissal.

Kate marched down the hall toward an exit. Naomi followed. Trudging after them and trying to smother a cough, Liz didn't dare glance back. She'd probably never see Corinne again.

Well, that's one less guest to worry about. And one more online review to dread.

Corinne made such irrational demands. Her out-of-control rage was so different from the marble mask she'd worn until this blowup. She'd looked as if she wanted to kill someone . . .

Liz caught her cloggy breath.

If Coach had been murdered, Asher seemed the obvious culprit. But could Corinne have killed him instead?

If so, she wouldn't be the first bitter child to take revenge on a neglectful parent. But what did she have to gain? And when would she have even seen him?

Still, the way her gaze had knifed that photo, then Kate . . . Liz shuddered.

Coach's fiancée might need more than moral support in the days to come.

6

Liz, sitting in the medical office's dated waiting room, barely managed to bury her giant sneeze in her elbow. She furtively blotted her sore nose with a crumpled tissue. Huddled in her warm knitted poncho, Liz hoped that by attacking her malady early, she could beat it fast—no one likes a sick innkeeper. She closed her eyes and slumped back in her chair.

Honk. Hooonk.

The man blowing his nose sounded like a sick goose. She opened one eye.

Jackson Cross. Despite his red nose, he looked almost as good as when he was at 100 percent.

Knowing she looked terrible, Liz shrank into her poncho. Maybe he wouldn't see her . . .

"Hey, Liz."

"Um, hi." *Please don't sit by me. I can't promise something awful won't come out of my nose.*

He plopped his muscular frame into the chair on her right. "So what's your self-diagnosis?"

Liz tried to summon a smile. "Just your everyday bug. I'm hoping it's bacterial, so I can knock it out fast with antibiotics. What about you?"

"Sinus infection. My face feels as if I smashed it through a wall."

Seeing a gleam in Jackson's eyes, she steered their conversation toward the subject least likely to result in a date. "It's so sad about Coach Albertson."

"The whole town's feeling sucker punched." Jackson shook his head. "Not surprising though. Coach trained his players hard, but I don't think he'd run a mile since college. Maybe not even a block.

I know his friends tried to talk him into a fitness program, but he blew them off."

Dr. Sam's nurse poked her head out the hallway door and beckoned to Liz.

"Hope you feel better soon, Jackson." She sniffled and escaped just before another massive sneeze wracked her body. The new tidbit of information about Coach's health made Liz wonder if she could extract a few more while at Dr. Sam's office. Of course, neither he nor his staff would divulge specific information about their patients. But if Liz probed a little, might she learn something that would provide some closure for Kate? Something that would help her shake this poisoning idea and come to terms with her loss?

As the nurse took her vitals, Liz remarked, "Isn't it just terrible about Coach Albertson?"

"Yes, so sad. And so unnecessary. John always was stubborn as a mule, even when we were in high school. I suppose that's good in a coach. Not good in a patient. But you know men." She snorted as she changed screens on the exam room's computer. "Everyone knew he never listened to Dr. Sam. Wouldn't come for office visits or lab tests. We can only hope that after this other guys with heart problems will think twice before doing the same."

Heart problems? So the man had experienced earlier difficulties. A host of follow-up questions tried to form in Liz's stuffy head. But when the bearded, congenial doctor entered, she knew better than to ask him anything. A Pleasant Creek native, Dr. Sam was used to fending off inquiries from curious townspeople. Concerning the death of the high school's longtime coach, he'd probably be doubly cautious.

As the usual "stick out your tongue" probing and prodding started, Liz tried to think of a way Kate could learn the exact details of John's death. If only Corinne would share them with her.

Somehow, Liz didn't think that would happen.

Her own congestion was in the process of morphing into bacterial bronchitis, the doctor said. Good thing she hadn't neglected it. Handing her a prescription, he looked straight into her eyes. "You're not going to rest much, are you? So it's useless for me to tell you to."

Taken aback, she stuttered, "U-um . . . no. I can't. I have guests coming in the day after tomorrow."

"That's what I thought. Go to bed early and don't overdo it, if you want to kick this thing."

On her way back to the receptionist's area, she spotted Jackson entering an exam room with the nurse. She shook a teacher-like finger at him. "Now, do what they tell you."

He grinned. And honked again.

As she trudged to Bontrager's Family Drugstore to fill her prescription, Liz mulled over how lonely Kate must feel. While pretty much everyone in town knew and liked her, she had been closest to John Albertson. Liz resolved to invite her to the next Material Girls quilting session. Surely being among friends would help Kate with her loss.

If Liz hadn't known Ruth was president of the booster club, her drugstore's windows would have more than hinted at her inclinations. "Go, Team!" and "Fight, Fight, Fight!" signs as well as dozens of toothy owls plastered the glass. Inside, the five-and-dime atmosphere was charmingly authentic if slightly shabby. Ruth still kept her grandfather's cash register at the checkout, and a smaller version of his soda fountain lined one wall. Today the thought of a root beer float made her shiver instead of salivate. But she might grab a coffee there after getting her prescription filled, just so she could savor its 1902 decor: black-and-white tiled floor, tables with curved wire chairs, and a vintage marble bar with red swivel stools.

"Don't tell me you're sick too." Stan Houghton joined Liz as she took her place at the end of the pharmacy line. The police chief turned to hack into his handkerchief.

She nodded. "I think an epidemic has hit the town."

"Just a usual February." Ruth, wearing her typical baggy denim jumper, zoomed past to help the other pharmacist.

While Liz and the chief exchanged small talk, an idea tugged at her. She'd worked with Stan Houghton during her early months in Pleasant Creek when one of her first guests had been murdered. They'd continued to collaborate when several other difficulties had popped up, and they had become friends who trusted each other.

Dr. Sam couldn't give her details about John—but would the chief, given Kate's desperate state?

After receiving her medicine, Liz hovered around a greeting-card display near the store's entrance. She followed Stan out and fell into step beside him.

"I thought you had something on your mind." He grinned. "You had that *look*."

She returned the smile as they walked through Pleasant Creek's homey downtown. "No use trying to hide anything from you."

"Well, what is it this time? Did Beans dig up a mummy?"

"No." She struck the levity from her voice. "Right now, I feel like I have to deal with John Albertson's death. In several ways."

His expression faded to gray. "We all do."

"But none as much as Kate Linder."

She'd expected him to know about John and Kate's relationship, and his grimace confirmed it. "Nice woman. Hard for her to find him dead like that. A real shame."

"Yes. Especially since, if he'd had his heart attack any other day—when someone was around—Coach might have been saved."

"Well, yeah." The chief gave her a curious look. "But we can't arrange these things, can we?"

Uh . . . Liz blurted, "Kate thinks someone poisoned him."

Stan's bushy brows hunkered over his eyes, but for a moment he said nothing. Finally, "She's been through a lot."

"Yes, she has. Even before John died, she said he'd received emails threatening to have him fired. His truck was vandalized. Somebody even spray-painted her garage with graffiti to get back at him."

"I know. He reported those incidents, as he always did."

"This happens every year?" Pleasant Creek was such a, well, *pleasant* little town. That Hoosier Hysteria had a dark side seemed so wrong.

"'Fraid so. For every ninety-six hardworking, law-abiding people, there always seem to be four nutjobs. They take their craziness up a notch during holidays and, around here, during basketball season. Some are pretty smart. Leave no fingerprints. Guess they watch plenty of TV crime shows." He smiled mirthlessly.

"It sure sounds that way," Liz said.

"Things are a little worse this year because folks thought the team would reach state finals with that Amish kid's help. They don't like to be disappointed, and the team hasn't done much the last few years. But that's no reason to think someone murdered John."

Liz remained silent as she considered the chief's point of view.

His steely eyes softened. "I'm sorry for Kate. But Doc didn't find anything unusual, nothing to make me suspect foul play. Coach was overweight and had borderline diabetes, yet he chowed down on doughnuts at Naomi's bakery every day. No secret that he didn't always take his blood-pressure medicine but never turned down a cup of joe. Actually seemed kind of proud of that. Doc said that given the stress of his job, it's surprising Coach lasted as long as he did."

"May I tell her that?"

"Okay, though I'm sure Kate already knew about his health. Most of Pleasant Creek knows it." He cleared his throat. "Still, I'd prefer you keep our off-the-record conversation private."

"Gotcha. Thanks, Chief." Liz waved as they headed off in opposite directions.

"And, Liz? If you run into anything unusual, let me know right away."

What? Liz turned back to search his face, but the police chief was already gone.

———————————————————

"I heard you were under the weather, so I brought you chicken soup." Bundled against the still-frigid afternoon temperatures, Caitlyn stepped inside the side door of the inn and offered Liz a glass container. "My mom's famous recipe, guaranteed to cure colds, arthritis, and most bone fractures." She grinned. "But you don't look like you need it."

"It smells wonderful." Liz sniffed appreciatively. "Thanks so much. I am feeling better, which is good, since I have guests coming. This extra boost will make me jump out of bed early tomorrow and finish cleaning the last bathroom."

"In that case, give it back." Caitlyn's teeth gleamed as she laughed. "I *never* want to do housework."

After putting the soup into her new refrigerator, she invited Caitlyn in for coffee. As they chatted, Liz marveled once more that this twenty-eight-year-old with red-streaked hair and a silver stud in her nostril hung out with the Material Girls, all at least twelve years older.

Caitlyn seemed to thrive in their multigenerational group. She worked as a nurse in a Fort Wayne hospital. Caitlyn had already won recognition for her excellent care, and Liz didn't doubt she'd achieve much more during her career.

She would know the answers to Liz's questions that had flapped like invisible crows in the back of her mind since her visit to Dr. Sam's and her conversation with Chief Houghton. Liz said hesitantly, "I'm sure you get more than your share of people asking for free medical advice, but—"

"Go ahead and shoot. I'm a veritable fount of wisdom today."

"As always." Liz grinned. "Can you tell me something about the tests a doctor runs on a patient before issuing a death certificate?"

"That depends on a lot of factors." Caitlyn leaned against the kitchen counter. "You're talking about an adult, right?"

Liz nodded.

"If a doctor believes a death is suspicious or if families or the police raise questions, then autopsies are performed. As for tests—even then, autopsy docs stick to routine procedures, with lab tests that detect only a few basic substances. There are a gazillion different tests that can be run to detect a gazillion toxic substances, but none of them are cheap or fast. Most doctors don't order extra tests unless they suspect that a specific toxin contributed to the death."

Liz prodded, "So if an older patient with major medical problems passed away and his family doctor issued the death certificate citing natural causes . . ."

"A patient he knew well?" Caitlyn gave her a keen glance. "He wouldn't do an autopsy or tests."

Liz decided to come clean. "You know I'm talking about Dr. Sam. And John Albertson."

"I sort of guessed that. But I didn't want to be presumptuous." Caitlyn cocked her head like a bright-eyed cardinal. "So you have reason to suspect Coach didn't die of doughnut disease?"

"No, no. That's just it. I don't have any reason at all to suspect anything's wrong."

"But you sense it." Cradling her coffee, Caitlyn sat on the stool next to Liz. "Don't discount your instincts. They've been pretty reliable, you know."

"I *don't* know," Liz groaned. "I've been fooled before. But this time, I think I'm suffering from Kate-induced paranoia. Coach Albertson's death is difficult enough for everyone without adding unfounded complications."

Caitlyn's gaze bored into her. "Do you think Kate's grief is trumping her good sense?"

Did she? Liz drummed her fingers on the counter. She had thought so . . . sort of. Until she'd talked with the police chief and he hadn't completely dismissed the idea. But Stan hadn't said anything to imply foul play in John's death either.

"You're not sure."

Liz held her head in her hands and moaned. "I don't know what to think."

"Kate and Naomi are good friends. Has Naomi expressed any doubts about Coach's dying of natural causes?"

"No. I was sitting with her and Kate at Sweet Everything when Kate said she thought John had been poisoned. Naomi seemed to think Kate was reacting to grief and anger at the struggles Coach experienced this basketball season."

"Naomi knows her better than we do."

True. "After the initial mourning, maybe Kate will realize she let her imagination get out of hand. And I'll realize that out of sympathy, I did the same."

"Give yourself a little credit; your instincts have been spot-on in the past. I think we should keep our eyes and ears open."

"I'll shift my mouth into neutral, but watch and listen," Liz agreed. "You'll keep all this confidential, right? No one, not even the other Material Girls, must know what we've discussed unless we see some hard evidence of foul play. I don't want to start any rumors." Even a spark of suspicion could fuel a firestorm of gossip that would burn down the town.

"Absolutely." Caitlyn pantomimed zipping her mouth.

They shifted the conversation to lighter topics. This evening Caitlyn had a hot date with a resident doctor she'd had her eye on for some time. She asked Liz about Jackson. "Are you two going out? You should. We could even double-date . . ." Caitlyn arched an eyebrow in invitation.

"No can do, not tonight anyway—I've got someone else lined up." Liz grinned conspiratorially at her younger friend. "Naomi and I are going to Indianapolis for an early dinner and a play."

"You'd better not stay out late." Caitlyn, suddenly all head nurse, crossed her arms and eyed Liz sternly. "And take a nap before you go."

"I promise." Liz crossed her heart. "Naomi has to get up early to bake for the Saturday morning crowd."

"Crazy woman. To take care of a sick little kid or save somebody's life, I'll drag myself out of bed in the wee hours. But just so people can eat jelly doughnuts? I don't think so." Caitlyn finished her coffee and headed for the side door. "Have fun!"

Liz watched from the utility room as her friend tramped through the snow toward her car. Sweet, caring Caitlyn. She would stop at nothing to help the sick and hurting, and her compassion seemed to be limitless.

But she always shot straight. Liz had wanted Caitlyn to laugh at her vague qualms, to say that John Albertson couldn't have died from poisoning.

Instead, the embers of Liz's suspicion had been fanned yet again. Why couldn't anyone completely rule out murder?

7

Mmmm. The Moroccan lamb not only entranced Liz's taste buds with exotic spices but transported her to another land. Maybe not quite as far as North Africa, but Indianapolis was certainly a welcome change.

Most of the time, Liz had no desire to leave her new home. But after the past few days, she and Naomi craved an evening away. The flickering candlelight, arched doorways, and rich tapestries of this Moroccan restaurant in Indianapolis's theater district met their needs admirably. Each dish their waiter brought exceeded the previous one. The fact that he was tall, dark, and drop-dead handsome didn't hurt either.

After dinner, the elegant hundred-year-old theater—with its ornate woodwork, stained glass chandeliers, and heavy velvet curtains—cast a spell over them. The play they'd chosen combined exactly the right touch of comedy and pathos, though a petite actress with light brown hair reminded Liz of Kate. Afterward, Liz assured Naomi that she felt great, and they drove to Monument Circle, with its towering, century-old Soldiers and Sailors Monument. The clear, frosty night was perfect for savoring the sights and sounds of the city.

While they shared a piece of to-die-for triple-chocolate cheesecake at the South Bend Chocolate Company, Naomi said, "I hate to mention this, but I thought you should know—"

"Kate's all right, isn't she?" Liz interrupted.

"She's functioning, if that's what you mean. But she's afraid to drive alone, especially at night." Naomi shook her head. "Kate thinks someone's been following her."

"Does she have any reason to believe that?"

"Seems like it's only an impression—and she's obviously exhausted and stressed. But this is the second time this week Kate's mentioned it. So I told her I'd follow her home whenever I can."

Naomi's phone dinged with a text. She glanced down and made a face. "Mary Ann. I better answer this one."

While Naomi replied, Liz mused about this latest twist. Who would follow Kate and why? Now that Coach was gone, Asher had no beef with Kate, and Liz didn't even know if he was still in town. It was more likely Corinne's dislike had crossed the line to hatred. Earlier, Liz had seen her at the inn, but she didn't seem any different, just sad and withdrawn. It was also possible that Kate's depression had turned into paranoia. And paranoia, well, even the best of friends couldn't solve problems like that. Liz sighed.

Pocketing her phone, Naomi said, "I asked Mary Ann to stay with Kate tonight while we were gone. She just texted me that she was leaving Kate's because she'd settled down."

"I'm glad." Liz hadn't noticed the small knot between her shoulders until this news relaxed it. She hesitated. "She's been so upset . . ."

"And Corinne was so mad at Kate at the high school. For a minute, I thought she was going to tear her hair out in the hallway."

"She might yet." Liz set down her gooey fork. *So much for a night off.*

Naomi did likewise. "Is Corinne still staying with you, or did she storm off to stay in her dad's house?"

"She hasn't canceled—at least not yet. I haven't talked to her, but that's not unusual. She comes and goes without saying much to anyone. Losing a parent is hard." *Unless she wanted him dead.*

"Difficult even without the excess baggage. How I wish Coach had worked some of this out before he died. And his will might make things worse."

"His will?" Liz stared. "How do you know about Coach's will?"

"That's what I wanted to tell you." Naomi's cheeks pinked.

"This afternoon Corinne and Coach's lawyer had lattes and scones at the bakery. A few tables near them needed cleaning—"

"I'm sure they did." Liz chuckled. Though conscientious to a fault, her friend wasn't above a little eavesdropping.

"They were full of dirty dishes," Naomi protested. "Anyway, I overheard part of their conversation. Corinne didn't raise her voice, but she seemed as angry as when she'd confronted Kate—her face turned that weird purple color and she sort of radiated rage. It was about Coach's life insurance beneficiary, and it's not Corinne."

"No name?" *Though I don't have to guess long to figure that one out.*

"Nope." Naomi's lip curled. "Of course, it's Kate."

Liz toyed with the dessert again. "Did they mention an amount?"

"No, though the lawyer told Corinne she'd receive the majority of Coach's estate."

"I can't imagine she needs his money, though you never know. However, I have a feeling that's not the issue. If Coach had left Kate a five-dollar Walmart gift card, Corinne would object. Did she mention contesting the will?"

"I didn't hear that. But then, I didn't hear everything." A wry grin tugged at her mouth. "Maybe I should have told them to speak up."

"Why didn't you?" Laughing for a moment felt good. But she shared Naomi's concern. This additional reason for Corinne's hostility toward Kate might make both heirs snap.

Naomi's chuckle quieted too. "What can we do?"

Liz picked up her fork. "Well, first I'm going to have more cheesecake. I always think better with chocolate."

Naomi gouged out a large, luscious bite in solidarity. "I don't get many chances to eat something I haven't baked."

Without further ado, they dispatched the cheesecake.

Walking back to the parking garage, Liz said, "Kate is closer to you, but I'll be glad to support her however I can."

"I've really appreciated your help. She's never been social, so she has few friends. But I can't devote all my free time to her."

"What free time? I've never seen anyone put in the hours you do." Liz shook a finger at her friend. "How many months since you had an evening out like this?"

"Touché." Naomi made a face. "But Kate's so messed up . . ."

"Mary Ann was willing to help this evening. I'll bet she and the other Material Girls would lend a hand until Kate can get back on her feet."

Naomi brightened. "I'm sure they would. We should invite Kate to our next gathering. As far as I know, she doesn't sew much, but she might come to one of our sessions to avoid being alone."

When Naomi shifted their conversation to other subjects, Liz happily followed her lead. At least they'd hatched a plan to assist Kate through her grief.

But who would help Corinne?

Despite Liz's budding suspicions, she was concerned about her guest's emotional swing from stoicism to unbridled rage at Kate. Was the coach's daughter experiencing grief? Guilt? Both?

Liz thought she'd left Boston for a simpler life as a small-town innkeeper.

But right now, people seemed more complicated than ever.

"Today Ruth would have flown the Banner Buzz." Mary Ann gazed out Sew Welcome's windows. For the first time since Coach's death, she'd donned her cheerleading outfit, now accessorized by a black armband. She scanned the brooding skies. "Ruth hasn't missed flying one in more than thirty years."

Liz, who had brought in coffee for Mary Ann and Sadie, would have loved to have seen her first Banner Buzz. "It sounded like fun. But the snowstorm late last night would have complicated things anyway."

"And Ruth's still trying to fit it in before the sectional." Mary Ann brightened a little.

"Besides, you've got Day of the Draw Monday. That should be enough basketball craziness for now." Sadie threw a sour look at Mary Ann's outfit, then withdrew to the workroom to fetch more quilt fabric.

Mary Ann thumbed her nose at her partner's retreating back before chugging her coffee.

Sew Welcome was usually such a cheerful place, but today it seemed to have absorbed the sullen cold. Liz was trying to think of something upbeat to say when the door jingled behind her.

"Liz." Miriam Borkholder gave her the brief side hug Amish women shared with family. Her smiling face beneath her black *Kapp* replaced the absent sun.

With her cousin's greeting, Liz's own smile peeked from behind the clouds. "I can't believe you made it to town." The Amish open-topped buggies provided little shelter from weather, even when the roads were clear.

"Pish! Only a little snow. Perfect for the sleigh." Her keen indigo eyes searched Liz's face. "Put on your wraps and come for a ride with me."

"Now?" With six guests arriving tomorrow, how could she leave?

"Definitely now. You'll be busy the rest of the week." Mary Ann contributed her usual, unsolicited two cents' worth. But then, she knew Liz hadn't seen Miriam in a while.

"Go play!" Sadie yelled from the back of the store. "Go now!"

"Well, since I've been voted off the inn"—Liz grinned at Mary Ann—"I suppose I will. Let me tell Sarah where I'm going." Sarah Yoder Borkholder, Miriam's efficient young daughter-in-law, had worked for Liz since she'd moved into the inn.

"Wonderful." Amazingly, Miriam's smile increased its wattage. "I'll buy supplies and we'll go."

Liz climbed the steps two at a time. She found Sarah dusting the

Sunrise Room, one of the colorful contemporary rooms on the third floor, and related her plans.

Blond Sarah, dressed in winter dark blue, her usual spotless white apron, and a black Kapp, looked pretty and immaculate even while cleaning. Marriage agreed with Sarah; her green eyes usually twinkled, but she didn't smile easily. "Have a good time. I will finish the rooms before you return."

Liz harbored no doubts of Sarah's ability to manage. She cleaned rooms better and faster than Liz. Sometimes the girl made her feel as if *she* were the grown-up in charge. Today, though, that was nice.

Even nicer—the whisper of snowflakes on the hood of her down-filled coat and the quiet, empty streets. Liz climbed into the old sleigh and covered herself with heavy wool quilts, feeling as if Christmas had reappeared in February. However, no sleigh bells jingled as Miriam untied the horses from a hitching post in Liz's parking lot; her cousin's strict bishop restricted frivolous adornment for people and horses. Miriam climbed in. With a soft "Giddyap" from her, the horse trotted down the street.

The town, always quaint with its gingerbread-trimmed buildings, had donned a fairy-tale mantle of snow. The bare, dark-chocolate trees lifted frosting-covered branches to the soft, gray sky. As Miriam guided the sleigh down side streets that hadn't yet been plowed, Liz closed her eyes and tilted her face upward for snowflake kisses.

Once outside the town limits, Miriam guided the horse to country roads blown knee-deep in snow. She tied the reins to a hook on the sleigh and shifted toward Liz, seemingly careless of the road before them.

Catching Liz's look of panic, she said, "The horse knows the way home."

Better than a self-driven car, Liz admitted, as the sleigh glided through the pristine countryside. She and Miriam, nestling under the quilts, chatted about Miriam's family. She missed Isaac, her eldest, who upon marriage, had moved to Sarah's family's house, where the two would work and save until they could afford their own home. "But he's happy, and Sarah is such a good wife to him. A little bossy." Her eyes twinkled. "But Isaac needs a bit of motivation now and then."

Liz shared the latest news from Steve and his exploits in Kosovo. Because Steve was in the military, Liz spoke of him only in general terms to her aunt Ruth Hammel and her uncle Amos Miller, two of her mother's Amish siblings she'd discovered in Pleasant Creek. Miriam's pacifist convictions were as strong as her other Amish relatives'. *But with Miriam, I can talk about anything.*

By the time they reached Miriam's big white house, their chat dissolved much of the sadness that had corroded Liz's heart the past few days.

Philip, Miriam's husband, helped them from the sleigh and took charge of the horse. "Go inside and sit by the fire."

Liz appreciated his courtesy, though Philip's smile alone could have warmed her. Since she had helped clear Isaac's name last year, Philip had abandoned his hostility toward her. He had discovered that Liz was not such a bad influence on his wife, after all.

Grace, twelve, and Keturah, six, opened the door as Liz and Miriam stamped snow from their boots. Grace greeted them with the sideways smile Liz remembered on her late mother's face. The girl's resemblance to Deborah Miller Eckardt had proved an early clue to Liz's link with Miriam and her family. Keturah danced circles around Liz, pigtails flying.

Liz took the hot mug of coffee offered and sat on the lovely handcrafted but cushionless chair by the stone fireplace. Despite stringent regulations that limited Miriam's decor, she managed to create an artistic yet homey ambience, with rag rugs, kerosene lamps, quilts, and crockery. Liz shifted, trying to find a comfortable position. She loved visiting her cousin but missed the cushy sofas by her own fireplace.

Miriam served Liz a too-big slice of sugar cream pie, but she didn't protest. "Mmm, delicious."

Grace, Miriam's prim elder daughter, lit up like a candle.

She must have made this unspeakably luscious dessert, Liz realized. Impressive, especially because the girl had to regulate the heat in the big woodstove to exactly the right temperature. Knowing the Amish frowned on any compliment that might generate pride, Liz toned down her lavish praise. "Did you make this, Grace?"

Eyes shining, the girl nodded.

"Was it your first pie?"

Nod, nod.

From the corner of her eye, Liz saw Miriam suppressing a smile, but the proud mom couldn't hide her face's glow.

Liz patted Grace's hand. "You have observed and carried out your mother's recipe very well."

The time Liz spent chatting and laughing with Miriam and her family seemed like just a few minutes. Only when she checked her phone for messages did she realize that two hours had passed. "I should have driven. I'm sorry you have to take me back too."

"I consider it an opportunity to spend a little more time together." Miriam smiled and sent Keturah to the barn to tell the boys to ready the horse and sleigh.

"An excuse to get away from the house is always welcome this time of year," Liz's cousin half whispered as they pulled out of the drive. "These winter days, with everyone underfoot, I enjoy my breaks here and there. Perhaps we might take the long route back?"

"I'd love the scenic route. We've experienced a few difficult days at the inn as well." Though Liz wished she could avoid the subject of Coach Albertson's death and basketball in general, a chance to mull them over with Miriam might shed light on her questions. "Do you know Asher Hilty or his family?"

Miriam's smile faded. "Of course. They are distant relatives of ours."

Liz had suspected as much, since both she and Miriam possessed quilts made by their great-grandmother Esther Hilty. But then, almost every Amish family in the county swung from some branch of her family tree.

"I suppose you'd like to know Asher's story." A statement, not a question. "I'm not surprised, with all the goings-on."

At the sadness in her voice, Liz backpedaled. "If you'd rather not—"

"No, it's important you know the truth. Perhaps you can help dispel any foolish rumors among the English. They always crop up in situations like these." Miriam tied the horse's reins to the hook and stuck her mittened hands under the quilts. "From birth, Asher seemed a rebel. Once he entered his teens, he made friends with English boys and secretly learned how to play basketball instead of helping his father in the fields. Coach Albertson discovered his abilities and offered him a place on the team and a home with him." Her mouth tightened. "Apparently, he put Asher in contact with colleges who wanted him to play for them next year."

Seeing her cousin's rare displeasure, Liz wished she'd kept her mouth shut. But since she'd opened it . . . "I suppose Asher's parents were furious."

"I think Daniel and Mercy had anticipated problems during his Rumschpringe. But they did not expect this. Asher had never been baptized, so they were not obliged to shun him. But *he* shunned *them*. His own parents. He hasn't spoken a word to his mother or his father since he left their house in the middle of the night, frightening them to death until they learned where he'd gone."

Miriam frowned. "We Amish have tried to maintain the best of relations with our English neighbors, but Coach Albertson regarded himself as a sports savior and therefore beyond the accepted standards of behavior. He tried to recruit several boys from our community. He even attempted to remake Asher in his own image. That boy tried to persuade my younger sons to follow his example, forsake our way of life for a game."

The *thud-thud-thud* of horse's hooves echoed in the tense silence. Even the snow's answering sparkles to the sun's overdue arrival could not brighten her face.

Then Miriam said softly, "I forgive the coach. I am sorry for his death. I forgive Asher. I hope he finds his way back to his family. But the disruptions to our community are not acceptable. Asher's mother has to hide her tears, for his father has made it clear their son is not welcome in their home anymore."

Not for the first time, Liz's heart ached for her cousin and the close Amish community that suffered when a member defected. Surely Coach Albertson had crossed a line with his recruitment of Asher. But what about Asher's talents, hopes, and dreams? Not everyone wanted to plow fields behind horses the rest of his life.

Liz stammered, "I-I'm sorry I brought it up and ruined our time together."

"You have not. I am sorry to speak so negatively." Miriam shifted her shoulders, as if throwing off the invisible cloud that enveloped their sleigh. "What we need is a good finish to our ride." She untied the reins and slapped them over the horse's back. "Hee-yaahh!"

The horse bolted. The force of the takeoff slammed Liz against the high-backed seat, but she didn't care. They skimmed over the snow through sugar-crusted countryside, the brisk, delicious air whipping their faces. Miriam guided the sleigh off the road, then back on, off, on, in a wilder and more wonderful ride than anything found in Disneyland. When her cousin drove in wide circles through pastures, Liz laughed, her mirth fed by Miriam's giggles, which reminded Liz of Keturah's.

When Miriam slowed the sleigh and guided it to a nearby barn, Liz hesitated to say a word, afraid to break the spell. A boy about twelve greeted "Aunt Miriam" and brought a blanket and a bucket of water for her sweating horse. After he rested for some minutes, Miriam set out for town again at her normal sedate pace.

Silent for a while, she finally turned to Liz, more than a hint of mischief curling one corner of her demure smile. "I drove along the borders and through the pastures of my brother's farm. Enoch is a year younger than I. When we were young, we were inseparable. No one knew we used to race our ponies like the wind. We agreed then that as long as we lived, we would keep each other's confidences." She fixed her gaze back on the snowy road but not before Liz caught a traitorous sparkle in her eyes. "We continue to do so, though we only occasionally drive as we used to and rarely race."

You included me in one of your secret rides? Liz wanted this moment to freeze in time. That Miriam would share something so special with her brightened the day beyond expectation. Quieting her internal hurrahs, she said, "Thank you. I, too, will keep your confidence."

Miriam's sisterly glance answered, *I know you will.*

"Could you drop me by the front of the inn?" Liz hoped to share a few smiles at Sew Welcome before she finished final preparations for her guests.

White buildings often looked dingy in the snow, but the Olde Mansion Inn's brick-red siding contrasted beautifully with the fluffy layer that coated its bare trees, evergreens, and red-berried bushes. Liz let the storybook magic of castle-like turrets, gables, and white gingerbread trim seep into her soul. What a place to call home.

Miriam's usual serenity returned. "I will pray for *Gött*'s strength for you as you care for others."

"And I for you." Liz gave Miriam the quick side hug. "Thank you for today. Be safe going home."

Liz turned the front door's antique handle and slipped inside. As she'd expected, Beans was sprawled on his favorite rug. What she had not expected: a red-faced Sadie and Mary Ann squabbling in the foyer like middle schoolers at a lunch table. Neither gave her a glance.

"I tell you, Beans is sick." Panic laced Sadie's voice. "I think he has a fever. Look at his nose. It's dry."

Liz looked. Dry? Not even close. Perhaps his slime levels had decreased slightly, but that hardly qualified the bulldog for doggy ICU.

Beans shifted his left hind foot ever so slightly so it could receive the full benefit of his favorite sunbeam.

"He's fine." Mary Ann rolled her eyes. "I'm not going to help you carry this lazy dog out to the car for another unnecessary trip to the vet."

"Unnecessary? How dare you!" Sadie's nose turned fiery red, a "strike two" warning sign that Mary Ann had better back off.

She didn't. "I'm sick and tired of your obsessing every time he burps—"

"Ob-sess-ing?" Sadie spit out each syllable. "You talk about *me* obsessing? I'm not the over-the-hill cheerleader—"

"Over the hill?"

Liz sprinted into the rotunda, grabbed a bucket of flowers the florist had delivered, and fled upstairs to peace and quiet. If anything would take her mind off their discord, her favorite task of putting the finishing touches on guest rooms would.

During winter, Liz missed the bouquets Kiera Williams, her other part-time employee, assembled from the inn's flower gardens. Liz stuck a few cheerful daisies into an antique glass vase and set them on the dresser in the Amish Room. They would partner with the sun's tentative rays to welcome Jerry and Dorothy Klein. The Kellars and the Meyerses had reserved the simple but colorful Sunrise and Sunset Rooms on the third floor. All three couples planned to attend the Day of the Draw and spend a few additional days together at the inn. Then they'd visit family elsewhere in the Midwest and return for the sectional games.

The third-floor guests would share a bathroom, so Liz hauled more towels and soaps upstairs and arranged them in baskets near the bathtub.

She was standing back to admire the effect when Sarah entered, her forehead scrunched with concern. "Miss Eckardt, I wondered if I could speak with you privately for a few minutes."

"Certainly." Liz gathered her leftover supplies. "We can talk now, if you'd like."

"Thank you." Sarah followed Liz down to her apartment, declining the cup of tea she offered. "I don't want to take more of your time than necessary. But I hope you can help me. Actually, I hope you can help Asher."

"Asher Hilty? You know him?" *Dumb question. Everyone in Pleasant Creek knows everyone else. Especially in the Amish community.*

"Our families have always been close." Sarah twisted her apron's edge. "When Isaac was falsely accused and others urged me to break our engagement, Asher understood why I would not. He never wavered in his support of Isaac, no matter how bad things looked.

"Now the situation is reversed. Everyone is against Asher, both the Amish and the English." A spasm of pain crossed her normally controlled face. "Isaac and I secretly offer what friendship we can. But we live with my family, and my father would be very angry if he knew."

"So you know where Asher is? Is he still in Pleasant Creek?"

"Well, Coach Albertson had allowed him to stay with him after he got out of jail."

Kate had made it sound like Asher spent a night or two on the couch, not that he was living with the coach again. Liz wasn't surprised Coach Albertson had kept his generosity a secret, but if Asher had unrestricted access to the coach's house, that made Kate's accusations against him seem a little less preposterous. Not that he would have done it, but if he was staying there he certainly could have.

"Asher had only been there a week when the coach died. He didn't know Miss Albertson so he took off, and when he came back, she'd padlocked the doors." Sarah's eyes flashed. "Asher has been on the streets these past few days. But we keep in touch."

Between Liz's soft spot for parentless teenage boys and her maid's beseeching gaze, how could she say no to helping out a boy with no one else to turn to? Besides, getting to know Coach's prodigal protégé might answer her nagging questions. "I'll be glad to help, though I'm not sure what I can do. He's on probation?"

"Yes." Sarah dabbed at her eyes with her apron. "I hope he does nothing to violate it; jail only made him angrier."

Great. "Asher must understand that I can't change his legal standing."

"I'll make sure he does." Sarah surprised Liz with a hug. "Thank you. He fought with Coach Albertson constantly. But now that he's gone, Asher seems lost. He even spouts accusations at Gött." Tears welled in Sarah's eyes again.

Liz patted her shoulder. "I can try to be a friend."

"I think he needs that most of all." Sarah sighed. "Isaac and I can't even be seen with him."

The boy must feel completely alone. When Steve's parents died in a car crash, Liz had welcomed him into her life, although she hadn't planned to parent a child. Now, despite her reluctance, she couldn't bear to think of Asher's isolation. "How can I contact him?"

"You can't. I'll have him contact you."

No troubled teen boy wanted to talk to a middle-aged woman he didn't know. Guilty relief spurted through Liz. Still, she said, "Tell me anything about Asher you think might help me—and him."

Sarah reviewed the accident. Asher, who was driving a friend's buggy, had consumed a couple of beers. He ran a stop sign and collided with a pickup. His passenger had been injured and the horse killed. Though in the Amish community, Asher was known as a troublemaker from his early teens, he'd never been charged because of their reluctance to involve the police in community matters. But as an intoxicated eighteen-year-old who had caused injuries and substantial property damage on a public road, he'd spent a month in jail.

"Asher often acts without thinking," Sarah lamented. "I pray he will learn from this and turn back to his faith and family."

I'm supposed to do that? Liz barely repressed a "ha!" But she reassured Sarah as best she could, and the girl went home comforted.

Liz? Not so much. Her heartbeat sped from a trot to a gallop at the thought of acquiring hard evidence of the truth about Asher.

But another thought worried her: Had she just agreed to help Coach's murderer?

8

The front door chimes rang after lunch the next day, and Liz zipped down the stairs to greet her guests.

A color-coordinated older couple opened the hundred-year-old front door as Liz made it to the foyer.

"Welcome to the Olde Mansion Inn." Liz extended her hand and tried to calm her rapid breathing. "Are you the Kleins?"

Their smiles matched too. "Yes, we're the first of our group to enter this fair city." Jerry chuckled. "I guess I should say 'town.' Pleasant Creek isn't exactly Miami."

"Thank goodness." Dorothy Klein loosened her scarf. "I love Florida's weather, but it's getting so crowded, and the traffic is terrible. As we drove into Pleasant Creek, we saw a buggy. I love the pace of life here. Sometimes I wish we'd stayed."

"Especially this time of year." Jerry rubbed his hands in anticipation. "One look at the high school, all draped in orange and black, and Ozymandias, sitting above the front entrance—"

"Ozymandias?" Liz wracked her brain. The name had a vaguely familiar, term-paper sound to it.

"Ozymandias. Ozy the Owl." The man gave Liz an "are you for real?" look.

"Our team mascot," Dorothy explained.

"Thanks. I'm not from around here." Liz explained Pleasant Creek was her mother's hometown but not hers.

"I thought I'd heard that someone from Boston had bought this inn last year. So you haven't yet experienced Hoosier Hysteria," Jerry exclaimed.

Liz summoned a smile, reluctant to admit the version she'd experienced so far hadn't been exactly fun.

"Tourney time is great." Dorothy hugged herself. "You'll love it."

"Um, sure." Liz handed them their key and summarized breakfast times and coffee hour. "At four, you're welcome to join other guests in the sitting room for freshly baked cookies and hot drinks in front of the fireplace."

"Sounds wonderful."

Nobody could stay negative in the glow of Dorothy's dimpled smile. However, Liz sighed inwardly as the kindly woman grabbed the couple's two smallest bags. Liz felt she had no choice but to reach for a large suitcase. The inn had no elevator, and her back was already yelling protests.

"Take the other small ones, Liz." Jerry gripped the biggest case's handle and tugged another from the pile. "Hauling these will count as part of my cardio workout today. I'll need it if I'm going to do those cookies justice."

Jeff and Jeannie Kellar and Dan and Susan Meyers, equally delightful couples and Pleasant Creek alumni, soon arrived. Liz had invited Corinne to meet the newcomers during coffee hour, but as usual, she politely acknowledged the invitation and stayed in her room.

Friends since childhood, this group made the social time a pleasure, teasing about grade school crushes and groaning about long-ago algebra assignments. All wore fuzzy, neon orange socks. Even the Kleins ignored the clash with their navy-blue and brick-red ensembles. Jerry wore his socks inside out, and Liz couldn't help but question the significance.

"We all did it during tourney time when I was playing," he explained as he snagged another chocolate chip cookie. "Gave the team good luck. During the week before the sectional, we wore the same pair every day."

Ewww. Liz tried not to calculate how many pounds of air freshener she'd need this month . . .

"Well, you can forget that, Jerry Klein," Dorothy sputtered. "Or move to a different B&B."

"If he doesn't change his socks tomorrow"—Jeff Kellar elbowed Jerry—"we'll wrestle him into a washing machine for you."

Liz decided to ask them the question she'd been wanting to ask for days. "What exactly is the Day of the Draw anyway?"

Jerry's eyes widened at her ignorance. "Why, that's when the teams find out who they're playing first in the sectional. We're hosting the games this year, you know."

"It's so fun," Dorothy exclaimed, and the other alumni chimed in their agreement. "Before the draw, we gather at the high school and Eat Orange."

"Eat oranges?"

"Well, yes," Dorothy continued, "but more than just oranges. We 'Eat Orange.' Some healthy stuff, like oranges, carrot sticks, and orange pepper strips. Opal always brings orange-glazed chicken."

"I make orange marmalade tarts," said Mary Ann, who had just joined her old friends for coffee hour.

"They're the best." Jeff rubbed his stomach. "Wouldn't be Day of the Draw without Mary Ann's tarts."

Jeannie added, "Some bring orange Jell-O, orange sherbet, orange Creamsicles—"

"Okay, okay, I get it." Liz laughed. "I suppose Eating Orange brings good luck?"

Dan nodded. "Then we gather to hear the results of the draw and have a rally. Awesome!"

"You've got to come." Susan clasped Liz's arm. "But be sure to wear orange."

"And don't forget the socks." Jerry pointed to his own. "No one's allowed into the gym without orange clothes or Ozy socks."

If I'm going to be a Hoosier innkeeper, I guess I should participate. Liz hoped her peach-colored sweater would do.

Mary Ann, delighted at Liz's plans to attend, promised to bring her a pair of the fuzzy, neon orange socks in the morning.

Teasing and joking with the lively group, Liz found herself relaxing.

Until the subject shifted to Coach's death, Asher, and the current state of the basketball team. Thanks to the Pleasant Creek grapevine and Facebook, these alumni knew all the details and were eager to discuss the situation.

Liz didn't even want to think about it. She also didn't want to be reminded of her offer to help Asher. She hurried to retrieve another batch of freshly baked cookies and then tried to steer the conversation to local points of interest. However, unusually heavy snowfall had prevented many of the area's festivals and events. Rides in open sleighs like Miriam's didn't tempt tourists in February as they did at Christmas.

But her guests didn't seem to mind. Basketball consumed these people. Now they were arguing about . . . shot clocks? . . . and whether the tournament should be organized according to classes.

This conversation reminded Liz way too much of her ex-boyfriend's incomprehensible rants about the Boston Celtics. She didn't have to listen to Matt anymore, thank goodness. But her tourney-time guests would always feel strongly about basketball, and she was eager to embrace every aspect of her adopted hometown. Perhaps she should ask Mary Ann to give her a crash course in the game.

Liz took in the older woman's cheerleading uniform and gulped. No. Definitely not.

Instead, she watched the debaters' red faces and flashing eyes. They loved basketball enough to yell and pound tables—a good thing they were sturdy walnut—then giggle like children at their own silliness. Enough to stand, join arms, and sing the "Mighty Owls" song. Twice.

Liz stifled a groan. How many times would she hear that song tomorrow? The next two weeks? She didn't want to know.

The kitchen phone rang, giving her an excuse to leave before they began a third chorus. "Yes?"

A surly male voice said, "Liz Eckardt? This is Asher Hilty."

Her throat tightened in surprise and dread.

"Sarah Borkholder said you could help me." He sounded as if he were issuing a challenge.

Liz tried to inject a friendly note into her tone. "Would you like to meet for coffee?"

"I guess so. Anyplace other than this stinkin' town," he groused, as if this were her idea. "Can you pick me up at the clock tower tonight? Maybe we can go to Fort Wayne or somewhere. Anywhere." His voice cracked.

Tonight? When six guests had just arrived? But they were going out for dinner soon . . .

"Will around six be okay?"

9

As Liz drove to the rendezvous, Asher's cracked voice resounded in her memory, reminding her of Steve as a teen when he tried to play tough but couldn't quite pull it off.

Would Asher show? she wondered as she parked in front of the limestone clock tower. Liz rebuked herself for hoping he wouldn't.

However, a tall, muscular figure rose from a stone bench near the car. For the first time, a small stream of fear ran through her as she scanned the town square. Most businesses were closed. She saw no pedestrians. She'd told no one where she'd gone. Perhaps she shouldn't have planned to meet him at night.

Then she realized that Asher wore only a light jacket and a stocking cap in the freezing darkness. Liz reached over to open the passenger door and waved him in.

Hands stuffed into his pockets, he slouched to her car and slid into the passenger seat.

"Hi, Asher. I'm Liz."

He shivered, though he hunched as if trying to hide the fact. He grunted a sort of greeting as she turned up the heat. The boy's brooding good looks would have wowed any number of teen girls, but to her maternal eyes he appeared thin and pale.

How long had it been since he ate? Liz planed concern from her voice. "If you want coffee and a snack, we can go to Cuppa Comfort in Fort Wayne. But I'm a little hungry. How about a burger somewhere? Or pizza?"

Even in the dim light, she could see his eyes light up, though within seconds, his eyelids hooded any trace of enthusiasm. Asher shrugged. "Pizza, maybe. Antonio's?"

"Where's Antonio's?"

"Between here and Fort Wayne, right off the interstate. Don't remember which exit."

"Not a problem." Liz typed the name into her GPS with a flourish. "Lavinia, take us to Antonio's."

"Calculating," Lavinia replied in her clipped tones.

Asher rolled his eyes. No, he and Lavinia probably wouldn't get along. But Asher did say, "Nice car."

She hadn't thought to score points with him because of the Acura's bells and whistles, but she answered, "Thanks."

As they rode in silence, Asher slowly stopped trembling. Out of the corner of her eye, Liz watched him stretch his hands toward the car vents. *Where have you been sleeping? On that bench?*

She'd feared Antonio's would be a dive, with dubious standards of cleanliness and cheap, cardboard pizza. But Lavinia directed them to a cheerful, family-owned place. After consulting her dinner partner, Liz ordered Antonio's largest pizza with pepperoni and black olives, Asher's favorite, ensuring that he could take leftovers home.

No, not home. Where? She didn't know. At least he'd have his next meal.

Maybe not. Asher ate as only a hollow-legged, teenage boy could—and then some. How glad she was they hadn't stopped for a mere doughnut and coffee.

His pale face gained color. "This is good. Thanks."

She'd followed her mother's advice: Feed a hungry man if you want him to talk. Now what? Liz nibbled at her slice, then ventured, "You've lived through a tough month or two, haven't you?"

Asher didn't roll his eyes this time, but his glance said, *Duh.* "Not what I planned, that's for sure."

No, you probably didn't plan a nasty accident, dismissal from the team, jail, loss of your family, death of your mentor. She said carefully, "I imagine you miss Coach Albertson."

Asher's face reddened, his eyes moistened, and he swore. "He said he'd make me a star so every college in the country would want me. He said I'd play in the NBA and convinced me to leave my family and stay with him. Then he threw me off the team." Anger devoured any sadness in his face. "I'm sorry, all right? I'm sorry I ran that stop sign. Sorry I drank the lousy beers. I'm *sorry*."

Asher was almost shouting, and he didn't sound at all apologetic. Liz forced herself not to shrink from him. A large family in a corner booth gaped at the irate young man.

"Sorry." He gripped a handful of his blue hair. "I told the judge and my friend and my parents I was sorry. I told Coach too. Nobody seems to believe it."

Given his mixed signals, Liz wasn't sure she did either.

"Coach was sick, you know."

She nodded. "Heart problems, I heard."

Asher glared at her. "I tried to help Coach, even though he kicked me off the team. But it didn't do any good; I only made things worse. I'm the one who killed him."

Liz stared. When her stupefied mind and mouth finally connected, she said, "What do you mean?"

"I ruined everything. Stressed him out so he had a heart attack. I didn't mean to kill Coach, but I did."

She took a deep breath. "Asher, people may be mad about your actions and about losing a chance for the state title, but nobody is saying you were responsible for Coach's death. Everyone knew he'd been in poor health for a long time."

"You can't say for sure that it isn't true."

Liz summoned her lawyer voice. "*You* can't say it is."

What irony. Or insanity? Was she really trying to assure her number one suspect that there was no basis to think he'd killed his coach? *I'm so confused . . .*

Something like a wave of relief crossed his face. He ducked his head. A few moments later, he picked up a pizza slice.

So, was that the remorse she'd read in his face at the funeral? Had he really thought he'd given Coach Albertson a heart attack?

Or could this kid be playing her? Playing everyone to stay out of trouble? Ingenious, if true. Way beyond ingenious. Well, according to Ruth, he'd weaseled his way into living at Coach's house for free before the accident. Sarah had told Liz that after Asher had been freed, he'd lived with Coach for a week or so before his death. Even Kate had acknowledged he'd been in Coach's house after his jail stint. So Asher had had ready access to Coach's food and his medicines. A few poisoning lessons from the Internet, and the boy could have wreaked vengeance on the man who had raised his hopes, then ruined not just his basketball career but his future.

Again, she scolded her presumptuous intuition. *I don't even know that Coach was murdered.*

Asher said little after that exchange; he simply ate most of the pizza. Liz, on a fake trip to the ladies' room, ordered two meatball subs to carry out. They might ease his hunger for a day. But as far as she could tell the kid was homeless. Her conscience reminded her that there were empty rooms at the inn.

Then she pictured Mary Ann and Ruth doing cheers and censuring Asher for his part in their beloved team's problems. The trophy-hungry alumni, clashing daily about all things basketball. Corinne's tight-lipped grief and anger at her father.

Was she going to offer a free room to Asher, whose presence would torch the others' simmering resentments?

To a boy who might be a murderer?

Driving back to Pleasant Creek, Liz wrestled with her thoughts so she hardly saw the road.

"Hey, you passed our exit." Asher pointed.

"Recalculating." Lavinia expressed her disapproval.

Asher snickered.

I guess they could get along. Liz turned off the GPS. If only she could switch off the ideas that messed with her head.

Even if she managed to keep the peace, did she really want to house a teen? He'd probably eat his messy meatball sandwiches while sprawled on her antique, hand-tatted lace pillows.

But the only option was to drop him off at the clock tower, possibly to sleep on a snowy bench in subfreezing weather.

If she didn't help him, who would?

Asher was right. Everyone had something against him.

Everyone but Liz. And anyone else who didn't care about basketball.

Sadie.

Liz gripped the steering wheel. While Sadie certainly didn't approve of Asher's behavior, she didn't give a hoot about basketball or public opinion. Despite her tough and often obnoxious exterior, she possessed a caring heart and believed in second chances. She'd invited her nephew to live on her farm awhile after his release from prison.

Would she be willing to give Asher a break?

Liz stopped at the grocery, leaving Asher in the car. She dashed inside and headed to a quiet corner of the store, where she pulled out her phone. Breathing a prayer, she hit speed dial. "Sadie?"

"Hey, girl. Whatcha want?"

A mechanical roar nearly drowned her words. Sadie's tractor, Liz guessed. Her friend often tinkered with machinery at night. "I need to talk to you about something important." She tried to keep her voice down because the produce guy was casting odd glances at her while he dumped peppers into bins.

"Speak up. Can hardly hear you."

"Sadie!" Liz shouted. "Can you turn off the tractor for a second?"

Finally. Now what? *Sadie, how would you like to take in a homeless teen with an attitude and possible homicidal tendencies?*

"Well, hurry up. Don't have all night."

Sadie wasn't making this easy, so Liz took a deep breath and told her about Asher's situation in one long burst. "I'd take him home myself, but we'd have a massacre sooner, not later."

To Sadie's credit, she didn't hang up. Instead, she barely hesitated. "Bring that boy here. Nobody's going to sleep on a park bench in this town while I'm alive and kicking."

But taking Asher in might prove far more difficult than Sadie knew. Liz's conscience jabbed her again. "Maybe we should think this through. Newscasts are full of stories of teens who prey on older people who help them—"

"You think I can't take care of myself?"

"No. I mean, yes. I mean—"

"If he gives me trouble, he's out of here. But I'll give him a chance. Bring him." She hung up.

As Liz darted up and down aisles, snatching a few groceries, she remembered Sadie's wiry, farm-wife strength. She'd once wielded a shovel, leveling a criminal. She kept a loaded gun at her bedside. And she knew how to use it.

Maybe I should fear for Asher's *safety.*

Liz paid and headed for her car. Would she have to sell this idea to Asher?

No. Asher tried to mask his emotions, but his eyes gleamed at the mention of sleeping inside. In a real bed.

Driving to the farm, Liz cautioned, "Sadie works hard, and she'll expect you to help in exchange for room and board."

Asher stiffened. "I know about farms."

Liz said no more.

As she guided the Acura into the driveway, Sadie popped out the big white house's back door. "It's cold. Get in here. But take off your shoes in the mudroom."

After introductions, Liz handed her the groceries.

Sadie deposited the bags in the kitchen as she hustled them into her cozy living room. "Sit by the fire and thaw out."

Asher sank into an overstuffed chair and stuck his big feet close to the fire. He blinked like a tired baby. Blinked again, as he fought sleep. He looked harmless and vulnerable.

Sadie offered them walnut cake made with nuts from her own trees. Still full of pizza, both declined. Liz, who accepted a mug of decaf, exchanged small talk with her friend until a soft snore from Asher interrupted.

Sadie gave his shoulder a little shake. "You better head for bed, boy, 'cause I sure can't carry you."

A ghost of a smile touched Asher's lips.

Sadie showed him an upstairs bedroom and a bathroom down the hall. Still sitting by the fire, Liz could hear bits and pieces of Sadie's half-bullying instructions.

Sadie soon returned. "Poor kid's worn-out. I didn't think he'd take a shower before he hit the hay, but he jumped at the chance. Used to being clean." She nodded, mouth pursed like the grandmother she was. "That's good."

"Yes, it is." Liz only hoped that the boy's virtuous Amish background prevailed in his other habits. "I should go now. Thanks for everything."

"Glad to help." Sadie stuck out her chin. "Asher did wrong, and he deserved what he got for drinking and driving. But I've had about enough of everybody and their brother trashing that kid over a silly game."

So, Asher had had an advocate in Sadie even before Liz called her.

As she drove toward the inn, Liz hoped with everything in her that she hadn't just put her friend in danger.

10

Liz's peach outfit wowed her guests the next morning at their Day of the Draw brunch.

"You look like a *real* Owls fan." Mary Ann, who had joined them, gave Liz her stamp of approval—and the required socks.

A bit later, Sadie sought out Liz to tell her that Asher had gotten up early to help with the chores. "I'm having lunch with friends in Marion, so I can't stay." Her friend eyed her and half-growled, "You're going to the draw this afternoon, aren't you?"

"I want to see what it's like." *You're one caring lady. But lighten up, Sadie.*

"At least Mary Ann didn't talk you into wearing one of her stupid cheerleader outfits," Sadie muttered. Suddenly, looking past Liz, she froze. "Wha—?"

Liz turned to see Mary Ann coming out of Sew Welcome. She flung out an arm like a showgirl. "Ta-da!"

Beans ambled into view. He wore an orange cheerleader sweater similar to Mary Ann's, with four matching doggy stockings and little orange boots. Curly, carrot-colored locks framed his homely face. A pom-pom hat crowned his big head, completing the ensemble.

For a moment, Sadie fell dead silent. Then, "Beeeans! Noooo!" She whipped around to her grinning partner. "Mary Ann Berne, how could you?"

Liz knew she was risking her life, but she stepped between them and let Lawyer Liz's voice take over. "Mary Ann, shouldn't you have talked to Sadie about this? And, Sadie, you said Pastor Brad preached yesterday morning about living together in peace. Did you waste two hours of your Sunday? Work it out, you two."

She turned on her heel, walked into her private quarters, and closed the door behind her. But not before she saw Susan and Dan Meyers snickering behind their hands at the top of the stairway—and others joining them to watch the show.

Amazingly, before the draw, the two struck a deal: Sadie decreed that the Mighty Owl display in Sew Welcome would shrink to half its present size and that the school song would not be played or sung within hearing distance of the shop the remainder of basketball season. An exception would be made only if the team reached the state finals. In return, she would permit Mary Ann to take Beans to the draw in full regalia.

"She gave me the short end," Mary Ann griped to Liz, "but this year, I think it's worth it."

Liz rode to the high school with Mary Ann in the gaudy patchwork-painted Sew Welcome van, loaded to its ceiling with food. She held Beans on her lap. Given the temptation behind him, the bulldog behaved pretty well. He didn't even mess up his fake curls.

The school, as Jerry had promised, was draped with garlands of orange and black. A huge blimp-like creature hovered by the main entrance.

"What on earth is that?" Liz asked.

Mary Ann gave her that familiar "are you for real?" look. "Ozymandias the Owl, of course. Ozy."

Liz knew she was being silly, but as they walked past the inflated mascot, its bared teeth still bothered her.

Beans cooperated beautifully. He actually walked all the way into the gym. He delighted the orange-clad crowd of hundreds, enjoying his favorite orange-glazed chicken and a Creamsicle before settling under a table for a snooze. Despite the noise, he didn't move a whisker until Mary Ann roused him.

Why was she leading Beans onto the gym floor? The exertion

evidently drained his energy for the day as he dropped to the floor at half-court in his usual comatose position.

A bevy of cheerleaders clad in orange and black, wearing black armbands like Mary Ann's, clustered around him, squealing. "He's so cute!" They petted the motionless bulldog.

Ruth, resplendent in her own cheerleader outfit, joined the group. Mary Ann beckoned the girls to a formation behind them.

What kind of "spirit" display was this?

Mary Ann signaled the beginning of a cheer, the liveliest the squad had done so far.

Beans slept on, oblivious to the kicks and jumps that missed him by inches.

At the apparent end, all the cheerleaders voiced a crescendoed "Goooo . . ."

Beans opened one eye.

". . . *Owls!*"

He popped up onto his hind legs like a jack-in-the-box and bellowed, "Woof!"

Beans brought down the house.

As the cheerleaders dragged in the enormous, inflated Ozy, the crowd spontaneously broke into a three-part cheer, with half the women and girls yelling, "Ozy!" and the other half, "Orange!"

Shouts of "Ozy!" and "Orange!" alternated. The guys boomed, "Orange-and-black-and-orange-and-black" in rhythm, like bass drums. The sound increased until Liz thought Ozy would explode.

She tried to think how she would describe the scene to her Boston friends. They'd never believe it. She would post a video instead, though she doubted they'd believe that either.

When the principal held up a hand and asked for a moment of silence in the late coach's honor, the place quieted as if someone had pressed a button. The basketball team, all wearing armbands, stood at attention. Liz wished Kate had come so she could see the respect shown to her fiancé.

The principal announced that Nathan Clark, the assistant coach, had officially accepted the position of head coach. Coach Clark—the same man who had retrieved playbooks from Coach's office—walked to the microphone to cheers and a round of enthusiastic applause. Surprising, given the contrast between his skinny, scholarly appearance and John Albertson's imposing presence. But at the podium Clark morphed into a rabid warrior who held the horde spellbound, raising their decibel levels to even higher heights. His team jumped and yelled like players possessed when he swore they would make John Albertson proud as they played on in his memory.

Coach Clark, you could win the town's vote for president right now.

Then the principal and team captain joined him to announce the results of the draw.

Already on their feet, the crowd again fell silent. A different sort of silent. A fireworks-about-to-explode silent. Liz leaned forward on tiptoe with the others.

The team captain intoned in a deep voice, "Our first sectional opponent this year will be . . . Delemont!"

The gym erupted in a two-minute chorus of cheers.

"Glad we're not playing Wildton first. They're the worst," Ruth, standing next to Liz, explained in her ear. "Play dirty. Pull worse shenanigans than Asher's, and no one ever gets thrown off the team."

Later, as Liz helped clear tables, she remarked to Ruth about Coach Clark's passion and ability to stir his audience.

"Nathan's a great coach—one of the best." Ruth lowered her voice as she sealed leftovers with plastic wrap. "It's been hard for him. He's been waiting for the chance to be a head coach for years. But I happen to know that every time he applied elsewhere, Coach Albertson used his influence to keep him here."

Liz noted how players and townspeople clustered around

Clark, hanging on his every word. How much he seemed to be enjoying himself.

Oh no. Not another suspect.

11

S*crape, scrape, scrape.* From a window in the Rose of Sharon Room, Liz could see Asher was doing a passable job of clearing the sidewalks of snow. He seemed to be a good worker.

Liz had agreed with Sadie: She shouldn't leave him unsupervised at her farm at first. So when she and Asher had roared up in Sadie's pink Jeep—it could handle any weather—Liz hired Asher to shovel sidewalks, the parking lot, and a path to Jaynes Lake so guests could take winter-wonderland walks.

"Coach had a snowblower," he said when she'd offered him the job.

An Amish boy wanting a snowblower? She tried to keep irritation out of her voice. "I heard we don't usually have this much snow in Pleasant Creek, so I haven't bought one."

She didn't tell him it was on her future-purchases list, knocked out of the top spot by the emergency refrigerator replacement.

The kid possessed a gift for annoying people. Upon arrival at Sew Welcome, Sadie and Asher were already glowering at each other. Would this arrangement last the week? The day?

Liz tried to brush away her apprehensions as she dusted the French armoire. The Rose of Sharon Room hardly needed attention because Corinne kept it so clean. Not a spot marred the mirror. Had her guest cleaned her room before she'd left this morning to—do what? She'd left her smooth, dark green leather briefcase on her bureau. Flapping the dust cloth around it, Liz sent it flying, and the briefcase opened as it hit the floor, a few papers scattering.

Blast. Liz scurried to pick them up, wondering if her subconscious had taken over her actions.

She so wanted to know what went on inside Corinne's head. This might be her only chance to find out.

Don't look at the papers. They're none of my business.

She managed to avoid that, though she ached to see if they had anything to do with John Albertson's life insurance policy. As Liz tried to replace the papers in the briefcase, she glimpsed the edge of a picture frame. Had Corinne brought something from her dad's house?

After two seconds, she pulled out the frame and studied the photo of a young John Albertson, surprisingly handsome despite his perpetual bad haircut. He held a pint-sized, pigtailed, beaming Corinne in his arms.

So, Corinne, you're not just all about wills and inheritances and business. You might have hated him for neglecting you and your mom.

But you loved him.

———

"I make a motion that we, as the Pleasant Creek Chamber of Commerce, contribute to the Basketball Booster Club in Coach John Albertson's memory," Jackson Cross stated.

As he sat, Liz saw people nodding, including Mary Ann.

A man resembling an over-the-hill NBA star shot from his seat like an ill-aimed cannonball.

"Yes, Larry?" The chamber president set his jaw.

"You know what I'm going to say. I'm not in favor of this motion." Larry Madison spoke through gritted teeth. "Look, I'm sorry Albertson died. Sorry for his family, the kids. But he was a lousy coach. *Lousy!* Especially the past few years." An expletive-laden criticism of the deceased man's skills exploded from him.

Other members shot replies like answering artillery. The yawn-inducing chamber meeting erupted into a free-for-all, untamed by the president's banging gavel. Liz noticed that the cub reporter for

Pleasant Creek News & Views, who earlier had dozed off over his fried chicken, took notes and pictures as if an international crisis had occurred. Other diners at Mama's Home Cooking peered through the philodendron-covered frame that separated the dining room from the meeting room.

As if Pleasant Creek needs more excitement. Liz almost wished they would return to debating bacon choices for their next pancake breakfast.

Finally, the president, with a piercing whistle between his fingers, quelled the brouhaha. "Sit down and shut up, or we'll need to have an extra meeting this week."

Quiet.

Glaring at Larry, the president said, "A motion has been made to contribute to the booster club in Coach Albertson's memory. Do I hear a second?"

Several sounded.

Larry slammed his fist on the table and left.

All in favor said, "Aye," and the motion carried.

Liz followed her fellow chamber members out of the restaurant. A cup of tea alone in her messy quarters at the inn sounded heavenly.

Fingers brushed her arm, and she realized Jackson was walking beside her.

His grin made solitude seem less appealing. "I'm sorry things got out of hand today."

She smiled in return. "It wasn't your fault."

"Of course it was my fault," Jackson said cheerfully. "But I think Coach deserves recognition for all he did for our town. I played for him, and despite his rough edges, he was like a second dad to me. People forget how much time and effort he invested in our kids. In our community.

"Besides, I know this chamber bunch. Some played for Coach, too, and we'll stay loyal to him to our last breath. Others, of course, believe he should have been fired years ago." He shrugged. "Better that we all yell during one meeting than simmer for years. Though I imagine Larry will continue boiling. I'm afraid nothing's going to change that."

They'd been walking along the town square, with no listeners nearby, so Liz let her curiosity loose. "Coach Albertson's death doesn't seem to have diminished Larry's anger any."

"Several years ago, Coach cut Larry's son from the team."

"Well, that explains that." *To a basketball-crazy Hoosier, anyway. But he was still ranting and raving about it?*

Jackson half chuckled. "You don't think that's an appropriate reaction?"

"A slight overreaction, in my opinion." Steve hadn't played basketball. He'd run track and cross-country, but he'd endured similar disappointments. She'd suffered with him, but they'd coped.

"To give you a little extra perspective, Larry's grandpa played for Pleasant Creek. So did his dad. Larry was a star forward here and played college ball."

Liz winced. "So it's a legacy issue as well. His poor son."

"Brandon's fine. Got a full academic scholarship to Butler."

"A shame his dad couldn't grow up too." The man's tirade still unnerved her.

She asked Jackson about his own basketball career and laughed as he described his world-famous position as benchwarmer.

A cell phone call from a prospective guest interrupted their friendly chat. Liz gestured in the direction of the inn and waved, surprised at the regret that tugged at her as Jackson nodded and walked away.

Her life overflowed with questions—questions about Corinne and Asher and whether they hated Coach Albertson enough to do him in. About newly appointed Head Coach Nathan Clark and his past thwarted ambitions.

And now, Jackson had unwittingly added to her sort-of-suspects list. Larry Madison.

———— //////////////////////// ————

Ending the call, Liz detoured to the library and searched newspaper files. She found an article about one of Larry Madison's contributions to the community. Then she found another and *another.* Liz read last year's newspaper write-up of Larry's leadership of the local Special Olympics committee. A picture showed the brawny man grinning, his arm around a little athlete with Down syndrome. He looked so beneficent and friendly, and to be fair, Liz had never known him to be unkind or hateful, just a little too opinionated when their paths crossed at the meetings.

Maybe he was one of those people who appeared mostly respectable in public but hid his nasty side with well-publicized good works.

Had his venom spilled over into vandalism? Heartbeat quickening, Liz checked the list of Coach-related incidents she'd researched earlier and had typed into her phone. Larry's adolescent grudge probably had persisted even when the basketball team was winning. Had he keyed Coach's truck and spray-painted Kate's garage?

No. She slapped a hand to her forehead. Larry's factory website featured a picture-studded article about his acceptance of a business award at a conference in California on that late November date. And according to the photo gallery, he and his family had skied in Michigan's Upper Peninsula the week after Christmas when Coach's tires had been slashed.

The same week Asher had been kicked off the team.

So Larry couldn't have participated. But she still felt the heat of his malice toward Coach, a loathing that matched Corinne's for Kate. Had Larry's rage over the supposed injustice done to his son fostered enough hatred to kill Albertson? Perhaps he'd rationalized that the team and the community would be better off without the coach.

Walking back to the inn, Liz decided to ask Mary Ann about Larry.

Are Kate and I both going over the edge? Naomi had said the grieving woman continued her assertions that someone was stalking her. Liz hoped that talking to Mary Ann would help her figure out a few things. If anyone in Pleasant Creek knew who was for real, Mary Ann would.

At the inn's side door, she stamped snow from her feet, then entered the utility room, shedding her coat and changing her boots for slippers. Peering through Sew Welcome's door, she noted that Mary Ann manned the counter alone. No sign of Sadie or any customers.

Mary Ann waved her in. "Some chamber meeting, huh? Sit down and watch the shop while I fetch *you* hot chocolate for a change." She jumped from her stool behind the counter and rushed off to the kitchen.

Liz stretched, loosening her neck muscles, and perched on a stool. Through leaded-glass windows, the afternoon sun shone its approval on dozens of colorful fabrics, pretty ribbons, and fancy notions, as well as finished quilts and other projects suspended along the walls. The completed scoreboard quilt hung proudly in the center of the shop, flanked by banners, pom-poms, and miniature stuffed Ozys, but Mary Ann's "shrine," as Sadie called it, was indeed half the size it had been, in compliance with their Beans bargain. Mary Ann seemed to be in a good mood, so they must not have fought about it today.

Mary Ann returned with Liz's hot chocolate. It was topped with twice as much whipped cream as she allowed herself and the chocolate shavings Liz reserved only for guests.

Ahhh. "You can make my hot chocolate every time."

"You work so hard. You deserve a few little extras."

Mary Ann's remark reminded Liz of her mother. Amid such a warm, fuzzy encounter, how could she probe her friend for information about an upstanding Pleasant Creek citizen? She sipped the creamy treat and murmured, "It's so nice and quiet in here."

"I wish Larry would get over Brandon's not making the team. He's a very gifted boy—but even in junior high, he wasn't basketball material. Dribbled the ball off his foot every time. Everyone could see it, including Brandon. Everyone but Larry."

"He sure hated Coach Albertson for cutting his son from the team."

"I'm afraid so." Mary Ann shook her head as she sipped from her own mug. "Some people just get carried away about basketball."

Says the woman with a whole closetful of cheerleader outfits. Liz gurgled and coughed until she could speak again. "I thought Larry would have a stroke today."

"I'm sorry you saw him at his worst. He's a good man who cares deeply for his family and for this town. He's done a lot to make it a better place to live."

"He just loses it during basketball season?"

"Completely. I think Larry aspired to play professionally, but he was mostly a sub during college. That still rankles, I think. Now every year, basketball brings on the same old grievance. Brandon doesn't come home weekends. And poor Angela—that's his wife. Larry's family just prays for April to arrive."

A festering, decades-old resentment had generated a literal March madness. Remembering Larry's purple face under his thinning hair, Liz could believe that this temporary psychosis might drive him to murder in the heat of the moment.

"I've really said too much." Mary Ann fixed Liz with her knowing gaze. "But then, you wanted me to, didn't you? Why?"

"I don't know . . ." Liz fiddled with her mug handle. "I just have a sense that something is wrong."

"Wrong? With Larry?"

Liz plunged in. "I can't shake the feeling that something's off about Coach's death."

Mary Ann's gaze sharpened. "What do you mean? Do you think he was murdered?"

Liz hesitated. "At this point, I don't know what I think."

Mary Ann set down her cup. "Look, I know strange things have happened over the past year. And Coach Albertson had plenty of enemies. But news flash! That doesn't mean he was murdered."

"I know. I know." Liz gripped her temples. "Kate believes he was poisoned."

Mary Ann frowned. "Kate also believes she's being followed, though we've kept an eye on her and haven't noticed anything unusual. Now she even says someone followed her a couple of times before Coach died."

Worse and worse. "So you think her grief has morphed into paranoia?"

"Possibly. She loved Coach very much." For a moment, the edge left Mary Ann's voice. But it returned in her next words. "Any reason you think someone would murder him?"

"Not really." Liz chewed her lip. "But when I talked to Chief Houghton about Kate's suspicions, he was a little ambivalent about the whole scenario."

"Of course he was. Stan's worked in law enforcement for decades, dealing with everything from jaywalking to murder, while keeping local politicians happy and juggling Amish and English culture. He's smart enough to never make conclusive statements unless absolutely necessary—and only when he has unquestionable proof.

"Aside from all that, Dr. Sam signed Coach's death certificate and declared natural causes. If Doc had found any irregularity, he would have said so." She waved a hand of dismissal, then rearranged a rack of buttons.

"If someone used a poison that mimicked the symptoms of a heart-related death, Dr. Sam might not have detected it," Liz protested.

"Some poisons are recognized only when specific tests are run, and he had no reason to be suspicious."

"Are you saying Sam Schneider didn't do his job?" Mary Ann's face turned as red as the apple buttons in her hand. "That's outrageous. First, you suggest Larry Madison might have murdered Coach. Now you think Dr. Sam neglected the final care of a longtime patient and friend."

Liz's lips moved like stretched-out elastic. "Uh—um—"

"I do sympathize with Kate. I'm sorry she's hurting so." Mary Ann shot her words like arrows. "But catering to her fears won't help her. Nor will putting down good, upstanding men who have served this community for years. They don't deserve to have their reputations ruined."

Mary Ann's uncharacteristically harsh tirade slammed against her. "I have no intention of ruining anyone's reputation. I have kept and will continue to keep my suspicions to myself. I've spoken only to Naomi and Caitlyn, and I talked to you because I wanted accurate pictures of Larry and Dr. Sam." She lowered her head. "I trust your judgment."

"Well, thank you for that." Mary Ann's tone mellowed a bit, and her cheeks faded to pink.

Liz felt emboldened enough to add, "If my 'lawyer's sense' proves wrong, I will be the happiest person in Pleasant Creek—unless we win the sectional, of course."

Mary Ann smiled wanly. "If wishing could do it, we'd have won state twenty times over."

"I wish I could guarantee that discovering the truth about Coach's death would be a win-win situation. But that might not happen."

"I still think you're letting Kate's problems influence you too much." Her friend crossed her arms, but her tone softened. "I don't believe John Albertson was poisoned. But I do believe in you and your integrity. I'll keep my eyes open . . ."

"And I'll keep my mouth shut," Liz finished.

"Deal." They grasped each other's hands.

Better leave while we're ahead. Liz touched Mary Ann's arm, then left to reorganize the pantry and do other tasks she'd neglected lately.

Despite their truce, she sensed Mary Ann's accusing finger still pointed at her. Mary Ann, who never put others down and rarely raised her voice.

Maybe Larry wasn't the only one who was overreacting. Since Coach's death, everybody seemed on edge. But was this a case of Hoosier Hysteria or something more sinister?

12

Liz turned on a heater to dispel the garage's oily-smelling chill and introduced her two high school employees. "Kiera, this is Asher Hilty."

"I know who he is." As usual, her taciturn employee said exactly what came to mind, nothing more, nothing less. Her catlike gaze fixed on the young man's face.

Asher dug the worn toe of his boot into the cement floor.

"Come on. I'll show you what to do," Liz said in the too-bright tone she'd abhorred as an adolescent. *Please, God, let them get along. Please.*

She'd planned for Asher to help Kiera with cleaning and organizing the inn's outbuildings. A good idea?

She'd soon find out.

Liz and Sadie had parked the Acura and the Sew Welcome van in the freshly shoveled lot so the two teens could work in the cluttered garage. Now she handed them each a page of detailed instructions she'd printed out to prevent controversies and keep her efficient gardener from being too territorial.

Kiera scanned it and turned to Asher. "Which do you think we should do first?"

Kiera? Asking someone else's opinion? *Should I put up a plaque?*

"Whatever you want is fine with me." Asher smiled.

What a smile. Liz hadn't seen it before. Oh no. Kiera usually didn't smile like this either.

Kiera pulled out her smartphone, the one luxury she'd bought for herself with her wages, and hauled speakers out of a tote. "You like U2?"

"My favorite."

She hooked up her electronics and filled the garage with "Fast Cars."

They bent over the worksheets, talking as if Liz wasn't there. Were they inching closer together?

Before she'd been intent on escaping the garage as soon as possible. Now she tried to think of an excuse to stay awhile.

———————— //////////////////////// ————————

At coffee hour, Jerry Klein stopped eating cookies long enough to point out the sitting room window. "Who's that tall kid out there?"

Liz didn't need to look to identify her teen workers laughing and talking on the front porch.

"Asher Hilty, right?" His face tightened.

The other alumni wandered to the window too.

"Yes. He's doing some work for me." Liz piled more cookies on the plates. Thank goodness Corinne had been gone all day—she wouldn't have appreciated seeing Asher on the premises either.

Jerry glared at the pair on the porch. "Would have been nice to have him on the team this year."

How could a person look so mad while munching chocolate chips?

"Jerry Klein, you need to get over this." Dorothy, his wife, sighed in exasperation. "Sometimes I wish there was no Internet."

"What's done is done," Jeff Kellar said philosophically. "So let's cheer on our team and have a good time. That's why we came to the North Pole, remember?"

They left soon afterward for a dinner with friends. Kiera finally left too, regretting that her homework wouldn't let her stay for the Material Girls' quilting session.

Asher joined them for pizza in Sew Welcome's workroom but begged off a quilting lesson.

"You can watch TV in my quarters," Liz offered. If Sadie could let the teen stay in her home, she could allow him access to her space for a few hours. Plus, there was zero chance he'd run into Corinne there. "Snacks on the kitchen table."

"Thanks a lot." Maybe relief made him polite. Or the prospect of eating again.

Liz turned back to the task at hand. Finally, an event and project that didn't involve basketball or the color orange. An inward "hurray" echoed through her as Sadie unfolded fabric for the Material Girls' spring project. The quilt they would make for May Day would feature pink, yellow, lavender, and bright blue tulip shapes alternating with triangles on a soft blue background. The other Material Girls fingered the various prints as if they were as hungry for spring as Liz. Opal had brought a potted blue hyacinth, and the women drank in its delicate fragrance. Soon they were talking about what they would plant in their gardens.

Naomi explained that Kate, whom they had made a point of inviting, had a karate lesson and couldn't come. Liz's jaw dropped when she heard their fragile friend had reached black-belt proficiency. Perhaps that would help her deal with her fears.

Liz had wanted to invite Corinne but refrained, worried about her and Kate both attending. Now she felt a pang of guilt, knowing that Corinne was alone in her room, yet it was so nice to have a gathering of only the Material Girls. Their group had always enjoyed guests, but they didn't mind focusing on their new project without stopping to advise or instruct. The talk and laughter flowed more freely too, as they spent a relaxed evening with each other, all mention of basketball temporarily banned.

In the midst of this peaceful lull, the inn's doorbell began to chime repeatedly.

Liz hurried to answer it, with Mary Ann on her heels.

Kate. She looked as gray as she had on the day of Coach's funeral.

"Come in." Liz slipped an arm around the trembling woman. "What's wrong?"

The other Material Girls appeared, Naomi rushing to her side.

"Someone slashed my tires." Kate spoke in a monotone. "I was going to drive to my lesson, and all four tires were flat."

"Let's call the police." Naomi whipped out her phone.

"I already did." Kate spoke as if in a daze. "They came. After I talked to them, I asked for a ride here."

Naomi threw her arms around her. "Thank God you're all right." She exchanged worried looks with the others.

Liz's muscles tightened. Apparently, Kate hadn't been imagining her stalker. "Would you like some tea or cocoa?"

"Tea," Kate said faintly.

While Sadie escorted the stunned woman to the sitting room, Liz scurried toward the kitchen but stopped dead in her tracks midway across the rotunda. Corinne had come downstairs.

"She did it!" Kate screamed. "She hates me."

Corinne halted, her face registering amazement, confusion, anger.

Liz grabbed her arm and ushered her toward the stairs.

Kate rocketed toward her nemesis and blocked her way. "What do you want? Do you want me to say I didn't love your father? That he didn't love me? Well, those would be lies."

"I don't want you to say anything." Corinne, a head taller, leaned down and said through gritted teeth, "I never want to see you again."

"That's funny." Kate's maniacal laugh sent a spiral of alarm up Liz's spine. "I just want to be left alone too, left alone to grieve. But you've been stalking me, harassing me. Now you've slashed my tires—"

"*What?*"

Thank goodness, Sadie and Caitlyn had joined Liz, wedging themselves between the two angry women.

"I. Have. Not. Slashed. Any. Tires." Corinne's eyes blazed, and she clenched her fists. "You're insane."

"*I'm* insane?" Kate resembled a terrier confronting a sleek Doberman. "You're insanely jealous. Who else would do such a thing?" She mimicked her opponent: "I. Have. No. Enemies." She stabbed the air with a finger. "Except you."

Liz held her breath. Would Corinne squash her like a bug?

"Kate and Corinne, this must stop right now." Mary Ann, wearing her cheerleader outfit, hardly resembled an authority figure.

But at her tough words, the wannabe combatants paused.

"You're both experiencing terrible grief," she continued, "but wounding others who are also hurting will only make the pain worse. Later, you'll be sorry, but you won't be able to undo those nasty words or actions."

Corinne glowered, then turned on her heel and stomped up the stairs.

Liz gestured toward the sitting room. "Kate, won't you rest in front of the fireplace? I'll get your tea."

Kate didn't budge.

Naomi gently led her toward the room. "Relax a little."

Someone needs to help Corinne too. I guess that someone is me. Liz glanced around at the remaining Material Girls. "Help yourselves to drinks while I get Kate's tea and take cocoa to Corinne."

Mary Ann nodded. "I'll handle it. I think we all need double whipped cream tonight."

Liz took beverages to Naomi and Kate, who, at least, had abandoned her fighting stance. Then she carried a tray containing hot chocolate with double whipped cream, some cheese, crackers, and grapes upstairs. She knocked on Corinne's door.

No answer.

"It's Liz, Corinne. I wasn't sure if you'd eaten."

"Please go away."

Liz had expected that. "No. I'm sorry, but I won't."

Exhaled frustration on the other side of the door. When it opened, Liz handed her the mug. "Here. Drink it while it's nice and hot."

To her surprise, Corinne sipped. For a moment, her features relaxed and she looked almost like that little girl Liz had seen in the photo.

She set the tray on a bedside table. "I'm sorry this evening exploded."

"I am too. Actually, I was planning to join you in Sew Welcome. I heard you'd be quilting. I didn't anticipate causing a problem."

What could Liz say? "We would have enjoyed having you sew with us."

"I would have enjoyed it too. My mom used to quilt . . ." The woman's eyes, now the color of ashes, matched her face. "I thought staying here would work better for me than my father's house. I was wrong. Maybe I should distance myself from this whole town. From everything. I'll find another B&B someplace else."

Again, what to say? With the funeral past and the will disclosed, why didn't she go home? Liz patted her arm. "I understand why you feel that way. But if you decide to stay, I will do everything in my power to ensure your peace and rest." *Including steering Kate elsewhere.* Liz sympathized with Coach's grieving fiancée, and the vandalism of her car was worrying. Regardless, Liz planned to recruit Naomi and the others to keep Kate from harassing her guest. *Corinne's innocent until proven guilty. I have to remember that too.*

"At any rate, I'll stay the night." Corinne picked up a cracker and added a slice of provolone. "Thanks for the food. I didn't realize I was hungry."

"Please let me know if you'd like more. Or if I can do anything to help."

"You've already been a tremendous help." A wave of emotion broke across Corinne's face. "I'm not sure I would have made it this past week without your kindness." She turned away—perhaps to hide her tears?

Liz touched her shoulder and left.

When she returned downstairs, she found Mary Ann, Caitlyn, Sadie, and Opal munching slices of Caitlyn's luscious apple-maple cake in the Sew Welcome workroom.

"Naomi took Kate home," Sadie informed Liz.

"Good." Liz helped herself to a slice. "Maybe when she calms down, she'll be able to think straight."

Sadie set her fork down. "Think straight? Naomi believes she might be right. That Albertson woman looked like she wanted to pull out every hair on Kate's head. And I can't think of anybody in town who would do such a thing."

"Whoa, stop." Liz lifted a hand and scanned the others' faces. No one was nodding agreement, but . . . "I'm angry too, angry that someone would scare Kate and slash her tires. But just because Corinne's from out of town doesn't mean she did it."

"They're both jealous over Coach," Caitlyn said, "still fighting over him, even after he's gone."

"Corinne definitely had a motive," Liz admitted, "but does slashing tires fit her personality?"

Poison would be more like it. The unbidden thought jabbed Liz's mind. Had she winced? Caitlyn was watching her closely.

Sadie shook her head. "Ms. High-and-Mighty doesn't seem that type."

"Do you know if Corinne stayed in her room all evening?" Mary Ann leveled her gaze at Liz.

"No. I was tidying in the kitchen after coffee hour, then after cleanup came here." Her heart sinking, Liz shrugged. "Corinne could have come and gone without my realizing it. Without *our* realizing it, since we were in the workroom till Kate arrived."

They all looked at each other. Not entirely friendly looks.

"I think we should let Chief Houghton work this out," said Opal, delicately touching her paper napkin to her lips. "We're all entirely too close to the situation."

"I know I am." Liz fell back in her chair. *One minute I suspect Corinne's a murderer. The next, I'm defending her—against a friend.*

Opal persisted, "We won't let this situation cause a problem among us, will we?"

Liz had grown used to Mary Ann's taking charge when the ties that bound the Material Girls frayed. But she'd never seen Opal, like a nearly invisible steel cable, keep them together.

Liz held out both hands. "I won't." *No matter what.*

Mary Ann grasped one of her hands. Liz stretched across the table to take Sadie's, and Opal and Caitlyn closed the circle. The friends formed an awkward but unbroken ring.

Would Naomi, Kate's champion, join in as well? Saying a silent prayer for their unity, Liz could only hope.

13

When Liz took Corinne breakfast the next morning, she wondered if her guest would be packed to leave.

Corinne, appearing cool and collected as usual, had decided to remain. "If the police somehow suspect me of vandalizing Kate's car, leaving wouldn't be a very good move, would it?"

I should have thought of that. Would Chief Houghton contact Corinne today? Liz pushed the thought from her mind. The day had started on a positive note. She wanted it to continue. "I'm glad you decided to stay. I meant what I said last night." *Both when I talked to you and when I held the Material Girls' hands.*

"I know." Corinne dropped her gaze and smiled when she removed the cover from her plate. "Bacon quiche and banana bread. Mmm."

Next Liz took coffee to Sew Welcome. The slamming of the inn's front door and Sadie's stormy face as she charged into the shop warned her the day was headed down the tubes.

Liz intercepted a sullen Asher and sent him out to shovel the lake paths.

"*That* does it!" Sadie smacked her Russian Cossack/Davy Crockett hat on the counter.

Liz jumped, as did all the notions displayed there.

"What is 'that,' and what does it do?" Mary Ann could have picked a better time to be witty.

Liz poured Sadie a mugful from her carafe. "Trouble with Asher again?"

"He's being a pain. But that's not what's hit the fan this morning." Sadie grabbed the steaming mug and chugged it. "Ow! Blast, that's hot!" Rubbing her mouth, she set down the mug and slapped an envelope onto the counter. "That came in yesterday's mail, but I didn't read it till late last night."

Liz and Mary Ann exchanged glances. Her friend picked up Sadie's hat with two fingers as if it were alive. She gestured for Liz to read.

Why do I get the honor? Nevertheless, while Mary Ann hung the furry hat in the workroom, Liz opened the slit envelope and silently read the profanity-laced letter, scribbled on cheap notebook paper:

Why are you feeding that Amish #&@?!! You actually let him stay at your house? He drove drunk. He ruined our chances to go to state. Get rid of him or you'll be sorry.

"Sweet, huh?" Sadie shook with rage. "I hate cowards, and idiots who won't sign their names to a letter are the worst kind."

The letter's writer clearly didn't know Sadie very well. Given her contrary streak, Asher might now have a permanent home, whether he wanted one or not.

Liz handed the letter to Mary Ann, who skimmed it. "You should show this to Chief Houghton."

"You better believe I'll show it to him. If the chief doesn't find out who wrote this, I will. Creep. *Scuzzball!* Some people care more about basketball than a homeless kid."

Liz tried to help Mary Ann soothe her irate partner. Finally, Sadie cooled down and called Chief Houghton.

Liz slipped out into the rotunda, attempting to regroup her thoughts. With Sadie's stress, last night's blowup, and the continual tension she'd endured the past week, a girl couldn't get a break.

The foyer desk phone rang, and Jackson's voice brought a smile to her frazzled face. She let him charm her into a last-minute lunch date, even suggesting the place.

Liz had way too much fun eating hamburgers and drinking

chocolate sodas at Bontrager's fountain with him. They inserted quarters into the antique Welte orchestrion, marveling at the way its piano, drums, cymbals, and tambourine played parade-type melodies. The early 1900s decor, the juicy burgers and fizzy, kid-like drinks shared with such a charming guy made Liz feel like the day might turn out okay after all.

She even took the opportunity to brush up on the town's basketball history. Maybe Jackson could tell her a thing or two about Nathan Clark.

After listening to a few stories of his own years on the high school basketball team, she asked if Coach Clark had played at Pleasant Creek too.

"Yep. On my team, as a matter of fact; we're almost the same age." Jackson shifted on the swiveling red bar stool that didn't quite fit his physique. "Nathan was the sixth man off the bench who could change a season. Basketball smart even then. We all knew he would be an awesome coach someday."

Liz stirred her soda. "I would think being an assistant all these years would be tough."

"I'm sure it was. But I never heard Nathan kick up a fuss. He was like that as a kid—accepted his role as sixth man and rocked it. Did the same assisting Coach Albertson, which I'm sure wasn't easy, considering he'd started out as his player."

According to Ruth, not easy at all. If both she and Jackson were right—which seemed likely as they kept their fingers on Pleasant Creek's pulse—and Coach Clark struggled with his boss, he didn't show any anger at his thwarted career.

Still, over time, his frustration might have built. To the point of murdering Coach Albertson? Sometimes even the "good kid" boiled over.

Or perhaps, as Jackson said, Nathan accepted his role and for whatever reason—loyalty to his hometown?—endured it.

As usual, her investigations produced more questions than answers. Liz barely kept herself from gritting her teeth.

Probably good, because Jackson was asking her out.

"I don't want to scare you," he said with his knockout smile, "but sectional games can get crazy, especially if you're not used to Hoosier Hysteria."

Why am I not surprised? "Crazier than Day of the Draw?"

"Absolutely." He upped his smile level to irresistible. "If you'll allow me to accompany you to the games, I will gladly risk my life to fetch refreshments at halftime. All spilled colas will drip down my back instead of yours, and I will shelter you from any showers of popcorn, programs, and/or rotten tomatoes."

"Sounds like I should wear a suit of armor."

"Going with me would be a much more comfortable alternative."

Why not? Liz accepted his invitation with a grin. "But I may not be able to attend celebrations afterward, depending on what my guests do."

"I don't think you'll have to worry about them. If we win, they might not show up until morning. Ditto, if we lose."

Walking back to the inn arm in arm (because of the icy sidewalk, Jackson said), Liz wished their time together could last a little longer. As they stopped to say goodbye in front of the snow-covered evergreens that graced a corner of the inn's yard, Jackson's gaze caught her glance and wouldn't let go. He leaned in . . .

A big snowball sailed between them and *plopped* against a tree.

Sadie's wicked eyes twinkled as she poked her head around an evergreen. Then a hailstorm of snowballs and accompanying yells filled the air. Realizing they were under attack, Liz scooped up a handful of snow and tossed it after Sadie's retreating back. *Splat!*

Jackson had already launched several snowballs at his aggressors, inn guests Jerry and Dan.

Jerry yelled, "Hey, Jackie! We may be old guys, but we still got it!"

Jackie? Liz knelt to collect more ammunition. They must have known the mayor from way back.

A snowball landed squarely on the back of her neck, its cold wetness trickling down her neck. She flung her snowball in the direction of Mary Ann's nasty chuckle. *Ha! Bull's-eye!*

And so the battle continued, with the alumni—all of a mature age—dashing around, ducking behind bushes, hurling insults, and pelting foes with soft, exploding white ammunition. Dorothy Klein proved a real gunslinger, and quiet Jeannie Kellar, who stockpiled snowballs in her stylish pockets, was a human cannon. Asher and Kiera arrived to find the chaotic scene and joined in the fray. Mary Ann fired ball after ball at Sadie, who tackled her friend, pushing her into a snowbank.

"You're ruining my hair," roared Mary Ann, who stuffed a handful of snow down her partner's neck in retaliation.

Sarah popped out the front door and chucked a perfectly aimed snowball that smacked Liz in the chest. Liz's not-so-perfectly-aimed snowball knocked off Sarah's Kapp.

"No snowballs to the head!" Jeff Kellar yelled. "Liz broke the rules."

"Get her!" Susan Meyers bellowed.

"I'm sorry! I didn't mean to!" Liz shouted futile protests as a laughing scrum of "friends" hoisted her above their heads and carried her, screaming, into the backyard, where the drifts were deepest.

"Noooooooo—" Her dissent ended with a mouthful of snow.

Sputtering and giggling, she dug her way out, then flipped onto her back and swished her arms and legs back and forth.

"I want to be a snow angel too." Jeannie Kellar sounded like a nine-year-old. She plopped beside Liz.

Even the guys followed suit, and soon a whole family of snow angels adorned the sunny, diamond-encrusted backyard.

"I bet that's the first time that kid was an angel," Jerry murmured to his wife, watching Asher flap his extra-long arms and legs. But Jerry was grinning a little as he said it.

Who would have thought that a snowball fight could act as therapy? For an hour, worries were forgotten as they played like children.

When they took a break to warm up in the four-season room, Sadie told Liz she'd taken the letter to the police station. "No fingerprints, the chief said. I'm not surprised. Maybe I'll never know who wrote it."

"Terrible," Jackson said, "and stupid."

The others, minus Asher and Kiera, who had resumed work on the garage, murmured assent.

"It would be nice if life could always be fun like this." The mayor flashed his famous grin, then sighed. "But the boss didn't give me a snow day, so I probably should go back to work."

Liz waved, along with the rest of the group. "See you soon." No way would she revert to the romantic goodbye that nearly happened earlier. Not with the Pleasant Creek grapevine monitoring their every move.

Dan and Susan eventually went back outdoors and rolled big snowballs. The others soon joined in to build a snowman. Liz would have liked to help them, but before coffee hour preparation, she wanted to drop in at Naomi's.

If only her friend hadn't had to take Kate home last night. Naomi hadn't joined hands with the rest of the Material Girls to affirm their friendship. Was she still feeling the rift caused by the Kate-Corinne blowup?

When Liz entered the warm, cheerful bakery, Naomi greeted her at the counter as usual, and Liz ordered a caramel latte. Since the few customers were focused on each other or their phones, Liz lowered her voice and told her about Sadie's letter as she took her first sips.

Naomi said the chief hadn't found any fingerprints to identify Kate's tire slasher either. "He or she must have worn gloves. He said it was premeditated, not your typical vandalism that happens occasionally during tourney time."

This news didn't remove suspicion from Corinne. Liz looked Naomi in the eye and said quietly, "I hope he catches that person soon."

"So do I." Naomi met her gaze without resentment, but despite Sweet Everything's slow time, she busied herself and didn't have coffee with Liz.

Sitting alone in a booth only doubled Liz's determination to keep their bond intact. *No way I'm going to let* anything *drive us apart.* She'd stop by Sweet Everything every couple of days. She'd offer to spell Naomi checking on Kate, for whom she harbored genuine concern. Somehow she'd demonstrate to Naomi how much she valued their friendship.

But she couldn't ignore Corinne either. When Liz brought her cocoa before coffee hour, Corinne told her that Chief Houghton had called and asked her to come to the police station.

"He questioned me." Corinne shrugged. "I would have expected that. But he didn't accuse me of anything. Just asked what I'd been doing that afternoon and evening. When I told him I'd stayed in my room, going through my father's records, he didn't press me, only said he'd known my dad and expressed his sympathy. Actually, Chief Houghton knew me when I was little." Her smile didn't reach her eyes. "I don't remember him at all. But he seemed a nice man, kind of like a potbellied uncle."

Yes, Chief Houghton played that role, all the while observing people's mind-sets and reactions, weighing possibilities. If only he would spill what he thought to Liz.

When the alumni guests showed up for coffee hour, they were dressed in thick, dry layers.

"Got to stay warm for the Victory Pickup Ride and the tailgate supper before the game tonight." Dan pumped his fist.

Seriously? After playing outside half the afternoon? Especially since . . . "This is just a regular game, isn't it?"

"Just a *regular game*?" Jerry pretended to keel over.

"I'm sorry! I'm sorry! Forgive me!" Liz faked panic, and they all laughed.

"It's the end of the season," Susan said. "Only two more games before the sectional. Pleasant Creek has to show what it's made of, build some momentum."

Amid the teasing and munching, Liz wove questions about Clark and Albertson into the conversation. The alumni confirmed Jackson's take on their relationship.

"Don't know how Nathan put up with that guy for so long, but he's been great," Jerry declared. "It's about time Clark got his chance to shine."

"I've never heard a hint of mutiny from Nathan's corner," Jeff agreed, "and no one would have blamed him for jumping ship."

Coach Clark certainly had the Pleasant Creek public on his side. But did the players, who had watched their daily interaction, see things differently?

No way could she talk with any present team members. She didn't know them or their parents.

But Asher might have an opinion.

Though he'd worked around the inn and she'd kept an eye on him, she hadn't talked to Asher much since their initial pizza rendezvous. Liz remembered how he'd relaxed as she had plied him with food.

With that in mind, she invited him to Mama's Home Cooking for lunch the next day, and the smile he gave her almost matched the ones he bestowed on Kiera. "Whoa, I love that place. Their chicken and noodles are the bomb. They even give you seconds on mashed potatoes for only fifty cents."

Later that evening as Liz ducked out on the porch to wave at a line of honking pickups stuffed with laughing, cheering orange-wearing fans, she thought that perhaps at Mama's, Asher would tell her more about Nathan Clark. About Coach Albertson.

About himself.

14

"If only we could be in two places at the same time," Dorothy exclaimed, giving Liz a goodbye hug while Jerry brought their car to the front of the inn the next morning. "I wish our kids had stayed in Pleasant Creek."

"I can't wait to come back for the sectional," Jeannie Kellar said. "Here, we can be kids again. But I don't mind growing up for a while if it means seeing my grandchildren."

"See you in a week." The convoy of alumni waved as they pulled away. They would drive together until they reached the interstate, then split up to visit family in Michigan, Ohio, and Illinois.

After they were out of sight, Liz combined forces with Sarah to take care of what required immediate attention at the inn. With only Corinne left, they could take their time catching up.

At noon, she found Asher, who was doing a surprisingly good job of organizing the tools in the garage. Clearly delighted by his lunch prospects, he bounded toward her like a big Labrador pup.

When they entered Mama's, Liz noticed a few diners whispering, and after they were seated, one couple moved to a booth on the other side of the restaurant. Bitter basketball fans? She and Asher ordered, and before long, he was digging into a mountain of chicken and noodles.

To Liz's surprise, Ruth, her lips stretched taut like string, made an effort to smile and say hello as she passed.

See, Liz silently addressed the die-hard fans who had moved. *As much as Ruth loves her team, she's trying to be civilized.*

Liz put the incident out of her mind and concentrated on maneuvering the conversation toward Coach Clark. "I heard the assistant coach—I guess he's the head coach now—speak at Day of the Draw."

"Yeah, that's Coach Clark." Asher swallowed a heaping spoonful of mashed potatoes. "He's a good guy."

"Everyone seems to like him."

He dug into the pile of noodles again. "Actually, I liked him better than Coach Albertson. Didn't yell at me all the time."

"Many say Coach Clark is one of the best."

"Yeah." Asher crunched carrot and celery sticks. "He is."

Liz curbed her mother instinct that demanded he chew more quietly. "I'm surprised he wasn't a head coach before now."

"Wasn't because he didn't try." *Munch, munch.*

Please stop eating long enough to tell me more. Liz forced herself to wait until the chewing subsided.

Her patience was rewarded. "Once, in the locker room after practice, I heard Coach Albertson talking on the phone about Coach Clark. He was lying through his teeth, man. Said Clark didn't pull his weight—late to practices, sometimes didn't show up. Said he had big holes in the way he taught defense." Asher snorted. "Coach Clark could teach college coaches a thing or two about defense."

"Why on earth would Albertson say that?"

He threw her a shrewd adult look. "He knew if Coach Clark went someplace else, we wouldn't be nearly as good."

"Do you think Coach Clark knew John Albertson was blocking his opportunities?"

"Probably. He's not stupid." Asher demolished another hill of mashed potatoes. "I don't know why he put up with it. Coach Clark really came through when Coach Albertson started going downhill."

"But I thought Coach improved the last few months before he died."

"At first, maybe. And, well, he tried; that's for sure. When he got to know Ms. Linder, he started eating more fruit and stuff. Worked out in the basement. Even got a plastic thing with little boxes to help him take his medicine at the right times. Still drank his coffee strong enough to eat your teeth away and never passed up a doughnut. And didn't go to the doc." Asher snorted again. "But he really tried to do the other stuff Ms. Linder wanted him to do."

"It didn't help?"

"He got worse. Must have got lots worse while I was . . . gone." He looked down at his plate.

You mean while you were in jail. At least the boy had the grace to blush a little. And to stop eating for thirty seconds.

Asher drizzled more gravy onto his mashed potatoes. "He didn't want Ms. Linder to worry. Fooled her pretty good most of the time. People at school too. But that last week, I had to help him walk some. Around the house. To his car. Twice, he got confused going from the kitchen to his bedroom. Seemed lost."

Liz bit her lip. If John Albertson hadn't been so blasted stubborn and consulted his doctor, he might still be alive.

Unless . . . unless . . .

Unless Asher's fooling me by creating imaginary symptoms on John's part. But why would Asher do that?

Maybe to try to hide the fact he poisoned his coach. Liz's temples tightened. Most teens couldn't invent such a story. Or carry off such a devious plot. Could Asher?

"So why're you so interested in coaches all of a sudden?"

For a moment, she found herself transfixed by unblinking cyanide eyes. She cleared her throat. "I'm still trying to sort all this out for Kate—Ms. Linder."

"Well, don't tell her she made him sicker."

He sounded sincere. He didn't want Coach's girlfriend to blame herself for his death, as Asher had.

Unless this show of concern was a façade too. Liz wanted to look away from his almost righteous expression. Could this be just another part of the big, big lie that was Asher?

———— *///////////////////////////* ————

All afternoon, theories about Albertson's death banged on Liz's brain like hailstones on a tin roof. She decided to escape with an evening walk by the lake. On the path, her boots crunched the snow's top layer. She inhaled brisk air and heard snowflakes blown by the wind against her hood. Nothing matched the serenity of a solitary winter evening walk.

The sun seemed eager to cooperate, splashing red and purple accents across the soft violet sky before it slipped beneath the silhouetted horizon. The pale moon had already risen in the growing darkness. Before long, stars, like many-faceted diamonds, would glitter in the black heavens.

Though Liz savored every season in her Indiana home, this winter walk along the secluded lakeshore nourished her spirit. Yammering voices in her head quieted, and she felt at peace among the trees.

Crack.

Liz jumped, then laughed silently at her skittishness. A raccoon. Or a deer. They'd grown quite brave lately, sometimes wandering into her yard. Perhaps she'd spot a buck, his antlers majestic in the fragile moonlight, or a doe and her yearling fawn.

She heard no further movement and saw nothing.

My toes are starting to freeze. I should have worn warmer socks. She'd walk a little farther, then return. Liz tried to tiptoe along the path, in case Bambi showed up.

Cra-ack.

Pulling out her pocket flashlight, Liz did a 360. Nothing unusual. No one else around.

Was ice on the lake shifting, as Sadie said it did sometimes? Part of her mind accepted this possibility. But for the first time, a jagged shaft of fear prodded her.

I'm letting Kate's troubles get to me.

But Kate had not been imagining things.

There's no reason anyone would follow me. No one knew I would take this walk. Even I didn't know I'd take this walk.

She should have told someone where she was going. She reached for her phone.

Blast. She'd left it at home, hoping to free herself from its tether for an hour.

Liz walked faster, her boots crunching through the snow. A similar sound echoed behind her. She whirled around, heart in her throat.

Don't be silly. Neighbors walk here. "Hello?" she called.

She backtracked two steps. "Who's there?"

Crunch, crunch, crunch.

Definitely footfalls.

Thud. Something hit a tree nearby. Snow fell on her in a sheet.

A dark, faceless figure crouched in a thicket.

Liz fled for the road without bothering to investigate. With the figure between her and the inn, it was the only direction to go. Heavy footsteps pounded behind her, but she didn't slow or look back.

She plunged through a small break in the woods and raced up the hill toward the street. Liz charged blindly across it, oblivious to the honking car that swerved to miss her.

Feeling safer under the streetlights, Liz sagged against the nearest thing. It was the barber pole in front of Barber Bill's shop. She clung to it, panting.

"Liz?" The delight in Jackson's voice died. "What's wrong? You look like someone's after you."

She gestured with a limp hand. "Gone, I think."

"Someone was really chasing you? Stay here in the light. I'll check it out."

She pressed her flashlight into his hand. He dashed across the street and disappeared.

Within a couple of minutes, he returned. "Didn't see anyone."

"Didn't think you would."

"I'm calling Chief Houghton." He pulled out his cell.

"I'm not sure that's necessary." Liz was feeling better and doubting herself. "Someone was probably just playing a prank."

"Right. I can see you're laughing your head off." His strong arm encircled her while he spoke quietly into his phone. Then he told her, "Chief'll be here soon. We'll wait in my store."

He walked Liz to a side entrance of Cross Furniture and flicked on the lights in his office.

She inhaled the clean smell of new wood. "Look, I'm okay."

"No, you're not." Jackson pushed his big swivel chair forward. She dropped into it. He filled a mug with water and stuck it into a microwave. "I know you don't spook easy. What happened?"

"I-I'm not sure." Her attempted laugh caught like a bone in her throat. "I thought I'd take a walk by the lake this evening. Things have been so stressful."

"I'm sure they have." A shadow of his usual grin appeared for a second. "Quite a mix you've had at the inn."

"Oh yeah." Liz sank back in the comfy leather chair as she told him about the figure in the thicket and the footsteps. As she talked, melted snow dripped from her hair. When she'd sprinted out of the woods, she must have looked like the Abominable Snow Woman.

Doubts niggled her. "Anyway, I thought someone was following me; I saw a person in the woods . . . at least I thought so at the time. But now I feel like everything that's been going on has affected my judgment. Somebody wearing earbuds could have been jogging. He wouldn't have heard me call to him. Or it could have been kids playing in the snow. Just fooling around."

Jackson seemed unconvinced. "First Kate Linder, now you.

Pleasant Creek has always been a place where a woman could feel safe."

After Chief Houghton heard her story, he shook his head. "Sectional time always gets a little weird, but this year . . . Do you know why someone would try to intimidate you? Because if he'd wanted to attack you, that wooded area down by the lake would be the place to do it."

"That thought crossed my mind a little too late to be helpful." Liz shifted in the big chair. "Well . . . I'm not sure."

"Not sure?" Jackson stared.

Chief Houghton crossed his arms. "You think John Albertson didn't die of natural causes, right?"

"What?" Jackson didn't sound that surprised.

The chief continued, "You've been checking out possible suspects, haven't you, Liz?"

"Sort of." Liz shrugged. "I've made no progress whatsoever."

"Someone may think you have." Houghton exhaled. "Tell me what you've found out, no matter how trivial or irrelevant it seems."

This might take a while. "First, would you let me use your cell? Maybe Mary Ann can bring me my phone. I left it at home."

"Don't do that again." Houghton sounded like he was joking, but she knew he wasn't.

"You don't have to call anybody. I'll get your phone." Jackson took her keys and left.

While grateful for Jackson and his rescue, she was relieved he left because she preferred to share a few of her investigation details with the police chief alone.

He didn't waste time or words. "So why do you think someone killed him?"

She slapped the chair arms. "I wish I knew. The guy had more enemies than Congress. But surely not more than your average Indiana small-town coach."

"True." Houghton surveyed her as if sizing up a case. "So you've gone with your gut on this one."

She forced herself to meet his gaze. "Yes. But I think it's more than instinct. Something—lots of little somethings aren't right. Though Kate's deeply depressed, she knew Coach Albertson better than anyone. From the start, she sensed something strange about his death, and that hasn't changed, no matter what her friends have said and done. We thought she was imagining someone was stalking her. But then some creep slashed her tires."

"Not to mention somebody chased you around the lake." The police chief frowned. "Can't imagine why someone targeted you though, unless they felt threatened."

She told him about Corinne's problem with sharing her inheritance with Kate and Corinne's behavior at her father's office. About Asher's love/hatred for his coach and his odd medical report about the man's last week. And about the way Coach Albertson had lied and blocked Clark's prospects.

"Sometimes I wondered about that." Jackson strode through the door and handed Liz her phone and keys. "Just how could Coach keep a talented guy like Nathan under this thumb? By giving him bad references."

Chief Houghton said nothing. But a calculating look crossed his nice-uncle face.

Liz mentioned that Larry Madison also hated the coach, but she suspected him to a lesser degree. "Do I sound a little paranoid or what?"

"More than a little." Houghton released a small smile. "Trust me, I've seen a lot of paranoiacs over the years; you're not that kind of person. Which, in my mind, raises at least a small red flag. Despite Sam Schneider's ruling of death by heart attack."

His calm, fatherly voice lifted lead weights from Liz's shoulders. *Maybe I'm not going crazy.*

"I agree." Jackson didn't hide his concern. "So after tonight, you must be doubly careful, Liz."

She flushed a little. "I will. But what do we do now?"

"Unfortunately, there's not a whole lot we can do, at least not officially." Houghton tapped a finger on his knee. "But I can think of a few folks I might talk to. Off the record, of course."

A slight grin surfaced on Jackson's face. It vanished just as fast. "What can we do to protect Liz?"

"Dixon and I'll check on her." The chief turned to Liz. "If we pop out of the woodwork or drop by the inn to drink coffee, you'll know we're just making our presence known. And we'll drive by a couple of times a night in case tonight's secret admirer shows up."

Look brave. At least try.

"I'll come by too. I don't wear a uniform like these guys"—Jackson grinned again—"but I'm a familiar face. This creep will know that someone's taking notice."

"A lot of your safety measures will be up to you." The chief pointed at Liz. "No more walks by yourself. No staying alone in the inn."

"Corinne's still here. And I can ask a friend to stay with me if I need someone." But given some of the Material Girls' doubts about Coach's daughter, Liz couldn't imagine that sleepover.

"If you sense trouble, here's my new cell number." Jackson scribbled it on a notepad and gave it to her. "Day or night."

"Same here. I think you've already got mine." Chief Houghton still sounded official, but his eyes twinkled.

Liz blushed. *Jackson and I are not a couple, Chief.* Going to the game with the mayor wouldn't erase the chief's impression. But tonight, she didn't care. Jackson's muscular arm around her shoulders and his consideration after her scare had felt very nice.

"You look tired." His deep voice exerted an almost lullaby effect. "Let me see you to your inn."

"You can come with us, Jackson," Houghton intervened, "but if you-know-who is still in the neighborhood, he needs to see a police car there."

Relief. Slight disappointment at not walking home with Jackson. *I am tired.* Liz pushed her weary body from the chair. *Too tired to figure this out tonight.*

She enjoyed the short ride home with the two big, solid guys.

But during the wee hours, the wind kicked up, tossing ice like gravel against her bedroom windows. She battled shadows while awake and dreams when she finally fell asleep, dreams in which she and John Albertson, wearing her peach-colored sweater and Beans's pom-pom hat, ran and ran through gloomy woods, screaming for help.

15

"What were you doing out in the woods alone last night?" Mary Ann demanded when Liz brought coffee to Sew Welcome the next morning.

So her all-knowing friend had already heard about her adventure. *Surprise, surprise.* Liz exhaled. "I wanted to take a little walk. Have some time to myself."

"I know." Mary Ann's tone softened. "But call me next time, and I'll walk with you, all right?" Her lips tightened. "You'd think it was the full moon last night. Not a good evening for several people. Kate, for instance."

Liz's ears perked up. "What's with Kate?"

"Well, you'd heard she was thinking of buying a gun, right?"

Wrong. Liz choked on her breath.

"She didn't, thank heaven. But when her father heard about the tire slashing, he decided to bring *his* gun."

Liz gasped, "He didn't shoot someone!"

"No. But he thought he saw someone running from her yard about midnight and accidentally shot out her lampposts."

"The world has gone nuts." *Poor Kate. First she lost John, then her tires were slashed, and now her lampposts shot out. Now she's probably trying to keep her father out of jail.*

"Stan Houghton cut him some slack. She went home with her dad to Michigan for a few days, mostly to keep him out of trouble." Mary Ann added coins to her cash register drawer. "I think a change of scenery will help Kate."

"Can't hurt." *Naomi needs a break too.* Between her ailing father and depressed friend, Sweet Everything's owner had been stressed beyond human endurance.

Liz said a quick goodbye to Mary Ann and dashed to the bakery, hoping to catch Naomi between customers. To Liz's delight, she joined her in a booth for a few minutes, and the two managed a friendly chat.

"I'm dying for another evening outside the town limits," Liz said. "After tourney time is over, why don't we run away?"

"Playing hooky sounds wonderful. Let's do it."

Walking back to the inn, Liz decided the day couldn't be all bad. Maybe things were looking up.

Her optimism lasted until the next morning, when freezing air led her to a broken window in the sitting room. A brick with a note tied to it lay among shards of antique glass. Liz hurt as if the splinters had sliced into her. Even if she could find glass to match the other windows, it would cost a bundle. She made herself look at the jagged hole, then she knelt and, using a tissue to preserve fingerprints, opened the note, handwritten on plain white stationery.

You ask too many questions. You're meddling in things you don't understand. Why are you helping Asher Hilty? He's nothing but trouble. Mind your own business or else.

Somebody has too much time on his hands. Liz speed-dialed Chief Houghton.

At Liz's news, the police chief's congenial voice hardened. "Be right over."

Corinne found Liz frozen in the sitting room, waiting for the chief's arrival. Witnessing Corinne's outrage at the incident, Liz could hardly believe she'd suspected her of being involved in Coach's death. *Either you have nothing to do with all this or you're an excellent actress.*

Moments later Chief Houghton arrived and, as usual, employed his we're-on-the-same-team approach, taking Liz's statements and reminding both women to keep the doors locked and their eyes open.

Afterward, however, over tea with Liz in her private sitting room, he warned her to remain cautious even while she was in the inn.

"You don't think Corinne did this." She was defending Corinne again, though she didn't know why.

"I doubt it, but she was on the premises." His shaggy brows lowered. "It's easy to think this note originated with someone who sees you as an outsider and doesn't take kindly to your helping Asher Hilty. But I think that's a smoke screen. What this person really hates is your nosing around. I don't like this. Especially after what happened at Kate's house and the high school last night."

"What happened at the high school?" Liz's mouth went dry.

"Someone got in and attempted to jimmy the padlock on Coach Albertson's office door."

"A padlock?" Liz remembered that Corinne and Principal Oaks had exclusive access to the office, but she didn't recall any padlock and was a little surprised that access was still restricted.

"Oaks told me that even after he agreed to keep everyone out of Coach's office, Corinne insisted she wanted to padlock it and keep the sole key. Oaks agreed to allow it for about a week. He played for Coach himself, so he gave her some leeway. Oaks figured it didn't matter one way or the other if the office was open, but then why would someone try to break in?"

No trace of the friendly uncle now. Houghton's eyes narrowed to slits. "I'm telling you this in confidence because I think last night's events might be connected—although Kate's dad isn't exactly a credible witness. And because I want you to be very careful. People who throw bricks are past using words to make their point. Don't take chances and don't assume they won't come back."

"I won't." Liz was still trying to shake off the shudders, but she wanted to know every detail. "Did the burglar get into Coach's office?"

"Fortunately, the perp couldn't break the padlock, but it sure was scratched up, and he took out a few security cams too. Maybe the night watchman scared him away."

Somebody wanted in Coach's office badly enough to attempt a burglary. Liz's heartbeat thudded in her ears. Perhaps trying to tamper with evidence that pointed to Coach's murder? But she was jumping to conclusions as usual. "Do you think students vandalized the school? Or teens from another school? I've heard these sectional rivalries can get pretty wild."

"Nope, there wasn't any vandalism. No spray paint, no graffiti. If rivals had been involved, they would have stolen Ozy or something like that. He's still sitting where he always does. Not talking though." Houghton's smile quickly disappeared. "The perp appeared to have a key to the school's entrances. Looks like he knew where the hallway surveillance cams were and broke them strategically. Then he tried to jimmy the padlock. He wore gloves."

Perhaps tracking down this guy won't be as hard as it seems. "A limited number of people have keys to the school, right?"

Chief Houghton rolled his eyes heavenward. "In theory, yes. We're working on that angle. But in a small town where people trust relatives and friends, they pass keys back and forth, even making copies of them. They don't always remember who did what, and the locks have never been changed on the school."

Liz could believe that. "Do you have any suspects in mind?"

"I might have a person of interest or two."

"A person of interest?" She started to smile at the euphemism, but his expression flattened it. "I don't suppose you'll tell me who?"

"Not yet. I've told you more than I usually share with crime victims."

"Do you think these incidents increase the likelihood that John Albertson was murdered?"

"They tend to confirm your gut reaction—and Kate Linder's—that something wrong surrounded his death. I *will* find out what that is."

———— ///////////// ————

Liz watched the chief drive away, wishing she could poke around

Coach's office and try to decipher motives for the attempted break-in. She could ask Houghton for permission to help sift through the mess when he got around to it.

Or she could ask Corinne to let her in now.

That idea didn't exactly fit with Houghton's request to tell him everything. Or his advice to take no risks. Corinne might have murdered her father, if indeed, he had been murdered. There was undeniably a lot of bad blood between father and daughter. One long-ago photo of the two of them didn't negate that.

If she told Corinne what she was looking for, Liz would have to trust her big-time.

Did she?

The pro-Corinne and anti-Corinne lawyers argued their cases in her mind as she cleaned up broken glass and taped cardboard over the gaping hole. She'd just started searching for antique glass dealers online when her phone rang. Sadie.

"I suppose Asher's come running to you." Her anger crackled over the phone. "Maybe he thinks you'll take his side."

Liz blinked. "Asher's not here. You mean he's not at your house?"

"He ate supper here, but we had a fight." Her voice faded. "I haven't seen hide nor hair of him since."

Oh no. "Asher didn't come home last night?"

"No. If Stan Houghton wasn't already looking for him, I'd sic him on that kid so fast—"

"The chief's looking for him?" Liz's heart sank down to her toes. So Asher was a person of interest. But where would he have gotten a key to the school? From another player who might have had a copy? From the coach when he lived with him?

Sadie spouted, "Stan believes he broke into the high school last night. What was that boy *thinking*?"

Oh, Asher.

"The chief knows the Amish have tried to deal with Asher over the years. He isn't backing down on this one. Asher's eighteen. He could spend years in jail for this."

Under Sadie's fury, Liz heard heartbreak. She steadied her own voice. "Does Chief Houghton know Asher's been spending time with Kiera?"

"He was headed to talk to her and anybody else who might know where Asher is."

"Would his parents know?" Liz might have met Mercy and Daniel Hilty at a barn raising or similar event, but she wasn't sure. And they'd never confide in an English person they didn't know. Maybe Miriam, emphasizing their Hilty connections, might help Liz talk with them. She told Sadie her plan.

"Asher hasn't spoken one word to them since he moved out, so I doubt it. But you can try." A slight quaver invaded her voice. "I'll be praying."

"Thanks. I'm praying for Asher too." Liz ended the call and headed upstairs. Before she left for Miriam's, she needed to touch base with Sarah about cleaning.

Halfway up, she stood stock-still. *Sarah.* Asher's good friend. Perhaps she knew where he'd gone. Liz found Sarah mopping the Somewhere in Time Room's adjoining bath.

The girl tensed when Liz told her about Asher. "The police are looking for him?"

"He may not have committed the burglary," Liz said, though doubts fluttered inside her like frantic moths. "But since he left without telling anyone, what's the chief to believe?"

From the anguish in Sarah's eyes, Liz knew she was reliving her husband's wrongful incarceration. "Asher should not run, whether innocent or guilty. Isaac and I can search the woods where we played as children or where they went fishing. If we find Asher, maybe we can persuade him to turn himself in."

"Thank you." If anyone could accomplish that, Sarah and Isaac could.

After a few words about cleaning, Liz drove the now-plowed roads to Miriam's farm. Sitting by her fireplace, cradling a cup of hot cider, Liz found it hard to believe Asher had come from a similar home. Fortunately, her cousin's daughters had gone to the barn to see a new litter of puppies, so she could tell Miriam about Chief Houghton's search for Asher.

Sadly, Isaac's mother understood how it felt to have a son in jail. "How well I know that sorrow. I would not wish it on Mercy or anyone else."

Liz hated to bring up bad memories for Sarah and Miriam, but they might help Asher make the best—and the hardest—choice in this situation. "Do you think Mercy and Daniel know where Asher is?"

"They would know of out-of-town relatives who might take him in. But they may not have even heard the news about the burglary yet."

Liz hesitated. "Would you help me tell them?"

Miriam's head bowed a little, as if she were praying. Or weighed down by the prospect. When she raised her head, she said, "It is better they hear this from us than from the police. But I must talk with Philip first." She threw on her heavy coat and ran to the barn.

Liz fidgeted and played with her phone, hoping Miriam's husband would approve their plans. Philip had come a long way in accepting Liz, but involving his wife with a boy who had served jail time and might serve more would definitely exceed his comfort zone.

The *clop-clop* of a horse's hooves and Miriam's shout brought Liz to the front door. Miriam, seated in an open buggy, waved Liz to join her. "The Hiltys will be more likely to listen if we do not arrive in a car. Let's go!"

Liz grabbed her coat and climbed into the buggy. This time, their trip held little of the magic she'd experienced during the sleigh ride. On this raw, slushy day, with wind slapping their faces, she wished the area bishop allowed covered buggies. The Hiltys lived only a few miles away, but by the time they arrived, Liz's face was brittle with cold, as if it would crack any moment.

Daniel, a tall, gray-haired man, took charge of their horse and extended a stiff welcome as the women exited the buggy. When Miriam introduced Liz as her second cousin, related to Ruth Miller Hammel and Amos Miller, Daniel's nods seemed less wooden but still far from welcoming. In a low voice, Miriam spoke to him in Swiss, the local dialect. Liz caught the word *Sön*.

The man remained expressionless and bowed his head as he drove the buggy to his barn.

Mercy, a petite woman with a careworn face, invited them inside. The Hiltys' plain home didn't reflect the artistry Miriam created in hers, but the big stone fireplace radiated warmth, with an old-fashioned coffeepot on the hearth offering a fragrant welcome. Miriam again introduced Liz, mentioning the twin quilts their great-grandmother Esther Hilty had made for their mothers as newborns, and Mercy warmed a bit to the connection. Miriam asked Mercy about their three older children—she'd told Liz that Asher was the youngest—and the woman brightened as she spoke of a tenth grandchild's imminent birth.

Daniel entered and sat, saying nothing.

Miriam folded her hands. "I am afraid I bring bad news."

The parents' faces stiffened into masks, as if they were used to shielding themselves from sorrow.

"About Asher, you said." Daniel spoke heavily.

Miriam said gently, "We thought to tell you before the police arrive to ask questions."

At the word *police*, Asher's mother covered her face.

Daniel said, "Go on."

Together, Liz and Miriam told them about the break-in, emphasizing that the police were unsure whether Asher had participated and only wanted to question him. Still, the couple's wordless distress pierced Liz to the heart.

When she asked them about relatives who might be sheltering

Asher, they reluctantly named a few in a neighboring county. These kin had, to some degree, left the Amish community.

"When they learn the police are looking for Asher, I doubt they will risk giving him refuge. His ties with them are not that close." Daniel had been looking at the floor, but now he raised his eyes and set his jaw. "If Asher comes here, we will not shelter him either. If he has done more wrong, he must face the consequences of his actions in the English world where he has chosen to live. Gött is not mocked." With that, he left, saying he'd fetch their buggy.

After the slam of their door, Mercy wilted. Miriam sat beside her, murmuring comfort in Swiss as tears poured down the other woman's cheeks.

Liz pulled a chair to Mercy's other side. If her godson were in trouble like Asher, she would be devastated too. If only she could ease this poor woman's pain.

Mercy's voice sounded as worn as she looked. "Asher has played the fool more times than I can count. Perhaps this time, his foolishness has caught up with him." A deep sob quivered through her as she grabbed Miriam's hand as well as Liz's. "But I fear more than that. I sense something terrible has happened to my child." Her voice broke.

Tears escaped Liz's eyes. Holding one of Mercy's winter-chapped hands, she prayed silently for the hurting mother, knowing Miriam was doing the same. "We will do everything we can to help find him."

"Dänka," Mercy said in a tattered whisper.

At the sound of buggy wheels and trotting hooves, they lifted their heads. Mercy resolutely dried her eyes with her apron. Miriam did likewise. Liz dabbed hers with a tissue.

She would not soon forget the couple's desolate eyes and stoic faces as she and Miriam drove away.

As they rode back to Miriam's farm, the wind battered them. Pondering Mercy's misery, Liz could not deny her gut reaction. She disagreed with Asher's parents and Chief Houghton. She didn't think Asher was involved in the break-in.

Then where was he?

16

"No. Haven't seen Asher for a while." The thirtyish relative who'd answered Liz's knock looked like Asher grown up—the wrong way. "If you find him, tell him he still owes Tim a hundred bucks, okay?"

Liz gave the man a smile and turned, letting the smile die.

"Sure you wouldn't like to come in and get warm?"

I wouldn't come in if this was the Ice Age. Liz waved and hurried to her car, gunning it to the main road. She called Sadie, who'd been knocking on other doors, but neither woman had found anything to go on.

The Hiltys had been right. None of Asher's ex-Amish kin had talked to him lately. Most appeared glad about that fact.

When Liz had called the chief after visiting Mercy and Daniel yesterday, he'd asked her to contact anyone interested in helping find Asher. They would meet at the police station this afternoon.

So after their knock-on-doors campaign, she and Sadie entered the nondescript brick building, rather plain compared to the downtown businesses that shared the Swiss chalet style.

Officer Dixon told them to join the others. Opal, Sarah, and Isaac already sat in the chief's office. Kiera sat beside Sarah, poised as if the chair could launch her.

Opal, who'd been using her deep-rooted connections in town, had tried to unearth witnesses. "I haven't found anyone who's seen Asher since you fed him supper two nights ago, Sadie."

"He ate practically a whole chicken. If he was worried about something, it sure didn't affect his appetite." Sadie half chuckled, then wiped her eyes. "He wanted me to take him back to town, and I told him, 'Why didn't you stay in town in the first place if you wanted to go to the movies? Gas isn't free, you know, and I'm not your chauffeur.' Well, one thing led to another, and he left, mad. He started walking toward town." Her eyes filled again. "I let him go. Why didn't I stop him?"

As if you could. As if anyone could. Liz encircled the older woman's shoulders.

"The ticket taker at the theater downtown says Asher and three other kids his age saw an action film." Chief Houghton, who had just entered, dropped into his squeaky chair. "After that, we haven't had much luck in tracking him. Asher hasn't been seen at the bus station. Or at any bus stations in Fort Wayne or surrounding counties. I sent pictures and his description to the state police." Pencils rattled as the chief drummed his fingers on his desk. "No stolen cars or horses have been reported around here recently. So if Asher left the county, somebody helped him—either drove him or loaned him a car or horse."

"Borrowing a car, he'd have to stop at a filling station sooner or later. Someone somewhere would have seen him," Liz pointed out. "A horse would have to be fed and watered. Even Asher's own parents aren't protecting him. I doubt other Amish would risk trouble with the police to help him. And his ex-Amish relatives haven't seen him." She shared about her and Sadie's contacting them.

To her surprise, her friend didn't chime in with her usual gusto. Sadie's silence said more than any outcry could have.

You're scared for Asher. I am too.

"Maybe he hitchhiked," Kiera suggested. "He talked a lot about seeing different places."

"Maybe." The chief exchanged glances with Liz and Opal. Most motorists would think twice and twice again before picking up a large, imposing young man with blue hair.

"I still think Asher might be hiding somewhere close," Isaac declared. "Kiera helped Sarah and me check some of the woods where we used to play together. Asher had his private spots too, where he hid when his *Vater* was angry with him."

Chief Houghton's mouth tightened as if he could well believe that. "Since you've known Asher a long time, you're bound to have more insight into him than I do. I appreciate your help."

His phone rang, and he barked into it. Apparently, no progress had been made in tracking down Asher. But neither had any progress been made in finding a motive for him to break into Coach's office. The more uncertainty reigned, the more unspoken fear echoed between Liz and Sadie.

What if Asher hadn't planned this disappearance? What if he'd been abducted?

Liz said little as the chief encouraged Isaac, Sarah, and Kiera to continue searching Asher's childhood haunts.

Kiera offered to canvass the high school. "They might tell me something they wouldn't tell you."

Opal reported the only scrap of information she'd been able to glean from her questioning of Pleasant Creek's longtime citizens. Her neighbors had driven past the high school late the night of the burglary. "The Appletons saw somebody drive a dark-colored car into the side parking lot. Could have been the burglar."

"Yes, it could have. A shame the school doesn't have money for cameras in the parking lots." Chief Houghton exhaled his frustration. "Thanks, Opal. I'll touch base with the Appletons. Perhaps they'll remember a few more details." He stood and thanked them all.

Sensing his dismissal, the others left, but Liz lingered.

"Something else, Liz?"

She summoned a coaxing smile. "I know Asher has been a pain in the you-know-what over the years, but is it possible that he's really in trouble?"

The chief grunted. "He's in trouble, all right."

"No, no, I mean—"

"I know what you mean." He shot her a patient but skeptical look. "You think Asher's a victim in this."

"I'm saying we should consider the possibility that his disappearance was involuntary."

He tapped on his desk.

Slowly, she admitted, "He's probably not completely innocent."

"You've got that right. When I talked to the kids this morning, one told me that after Asher was kicked off the team, he slashed Coach's tires."

The confirmation shouldn't have sucker punched her, but it did. "Why didn't the student come forward before?"

"Because he was afraid I'd think he was involved. Typical teen." He hesitated. "The kicker is that another high school student says he saw someone who looked like Asher at the school with some out-of-town kids."

Liz's stomach dropped to her heels. For a moment, she could say nothing.

"That's confidential, of course. I didn't tell the others because that witness isn't very reliable. He's been in trouble more than once, though recently, he's seemed to get his act together. I'm checking out his movements that night as well. Other students told me he and Asher have clashed several times, that they've never gotten along. He may have lied to get back at Asher." The chief leaned forward. "I'm trying to be fair."

Liz extended her hand. "I know you're working hard to keep Pleasant Creek a safe place to live."

The furrows in his leathery forehead smoothed a little as he grasped her hand. "Yes, I am. And that includes you. So if you hear from Asher, let me know immediately. For his sake and for yours."

She tried to unbolt her gaze from his steely one, without success. "I will."

***

Chunk! Chunk, chunk!

Liz leaped and grabbed at the darkness, then landed on her bed with an answering thud. "What in the world?"

A few more *chunks* and she realized that large icicles on the inn's eaves, loosened by yesterday's thaw, had hit the ground.

"I'm becoming a nervous old lady," Liz muttered into her pillow. She checked her bedside clock. Three thirty.

At least her manic brain had allowed her to sleep for a few hours. But now it interrogated her about Asher's possible abduction, Coach's death, the break-in, her smashed sitting room window, the slashed tires . . .

When she moved to Pleasant Creek, she thought she'd exchanged Boston's high crime rate for one near zero. Liz shifted for the hundredth time. With all the strange goings-on the past year, was she now seeing John Albertson's for-real heart attack through a whodunit filter? Maybe Asher wasn't a murderer because there wasn't a murder; he was just one more mad-at-the-world teen vandal who'd disappeared to save his hide after botching an ill-planned burglary.

Desperate, Liz took refuge in a twenty-repetition mental chorus of "Feliz Navidad." She'd taught herself this trick when worry about Steve in Kosovo threatened to drown her at night. Now she all but sang aloud to fight off her doubts, succeeding for the most part.

But one insistent little ghost poked her mind with an urgent but unformed message.

She pulled the pillow over her head and ratcheted up the chorus. *I can't think anymore. Don't want to think anymore. Coach John Albertson died of a heart attack, and Asher Hilty is a delinquent. End of story.*

Liz thought she'd stare at the ceiling the rest of the night, so she was quite surprised when the alarm woke her a few hours later. She hustled to the kitchen and prepared a scalloped potato, ham, and egg casserole for her guests and arranged breads and fruit on the buffet while the casserole was in the oven. Then she consulted with Sarah about preparing for the returning alumni. She was busy wondering whether or not to brew another pot of coffee when alarm bells went off in her head.

A vivid, sad picture of Asher's distraught parents in their tidy home flooded her mind. But she'd seen something else there, something that mattered.

What?

Something in Coach's office too. Liz shook her head as if to clear it. That tiny, windowless room reminded her of a *Where's Waldo?* picture, jammed with so much stuff, it was a wonder Coach could find himself. What could his overflowing office have in common with the Hiltys' spotless, sparse home?

She'd seen something important in both settings. She was sure of it.

If only she could remember what that something was.

17

Later that morning, Liz found two packages on the inn's doorstep, both addressed to Sew Welcome.

Odd. From the beginning, Sadie and Mary Ann, who enjoyed new sewing supplies as if they were gifts, brought in those boxes immediately. Even when mysterious, nasty packages had appeared on many businesses' doorsteps last holiday season, their enthusiasm for new deliveries never waned.

Were both ladies sick today? But the store's lights were on.

"What's up with this, Beans?" she asked the bulldog, who was spread out in his usual spot.

In answer, he turned over.

Did such drastic movement portend trouble at the shop? Liz grabbed the packages and rushed into Sew Welcome.

"Thank you." Mary Ann's face lit up.

"What happened to you?" Liz pointed at the medical boot on Mary Ann's foot. It didn't fit with her cheerleading getup.

"Oh, it's nothing. Slipped on a slick spot." Mary Ann cast an eagle-eyed glance at her friend.

Liz nodded, too tired to comment.

Mary Ann shook her head. "Dark circles under your eyes, just like Sadie's. You're both worried to death about that boy. I told her to stay home and rest."

"You told *Sadie* to stay home?" Liz countered. "What about you? What would Dr. Sam say about that?"

"He knows I won't let one silly little fall slow me down. Besides, Sadie insisted she would come in, just a little later than usual." Guiltily, Mary Ann propped up her leg on a stool. "You're the one who needs a nap."

"I would, if I thought I could sleep." A giant yawn almost split Liz's face.

"Then maybe you should visit your aunt Ruth. You always relax at her house."

Yearning coursed through Liz for her aunt's hug, for the voice that reminded her so much of her late mother's. What a wonderful idea. "I'll run over there for a few minutes."

"Good." Mary Ann shooed her toward the door. "Try to forget about everything for a while."

When her aunt opened her door, the joy on her plump face spilled onto Liz. Aunt Ruth threw her arms around her in a very un-Amish hug, sputtering her usual "you look tired child why must you work so hard?" welcome. Before Liz knew it, she'd been handed a large slice of dried-apple pie and ushered to a chair by the crackling fire.

"Coffee's ready." Aunt Ruth swept the pot from the hearth and poised it over a cream-colored crockery mug.

Liz sniffed appreciatively as her aunt poured. Seems as if everyone in Pleasant Creek owns one of those charming old coffeepots.

Everyone? Liz froze.

The blurred image that had dogged her suddenly sharpened. Where had she seen others?

At the Hiltys'.

In Coach's office.

"Liz, are you all right?" Aunt Ruth's forehead puckered. "Is something wrong with the pie?"

"Nothing's wrong," Liz assured her, though her stomach danced to a weird mix of a joyful "Hallelujah Chorus" and an ominous *Phantom of the Opera* theme. Somehow she managed a semblance of normal conversation for another hour—she could tell Aunt Ruth was steering it away from current events—while she grappled with her thoughts.

What is up with the stupid coffeepot?

Aunt Ruth poured me coffee. Mercy Hilty poured me coffee.

Coach certainly didn't pour me coffee. A picture of the booster club president in Coach's office, grasping the coffeepot, popped into Liz's mind. Ruth Bontrager had wanted to take the pot with her.

Liz choked. Fortunately, Aunt Ruth was describing her granddaughter's first attempts at reading, and she didn't appear to notice.

Finally, Liz kissed her aunt goodbye and made a beeline for the high school.

Faithful Arlene guarded the coach's office, still padlocked. Her eyes widened at Liz's approach, but she visibly relaxed when Liz assured her she had no wish to enter. "I'm just trying to figure out who would want to burglarize Coach's office and why—mostly for his fiancée's sake."

"None of us get that. If Coach had gotten the team to the state finals, I could understand why somebody might want a memento or something. With the losing streak lately, it doesn't make sense."

"No, people aren't lining up for souvenirs, though many miss him. Kate's still struggling." Liz sighed. "His players and assistants had a hard time at the funeral. Ruth too."

"Oh yes. Ruth and Coach went way back. She made his coffee every day, strong enough to pour itself—the way he liked it." A slight smile lit Arlene's sad face. "Those two fought like a cat and dog for *years*. But she brewed it for him every single morning, even when they were mad."

Liz lightened her tone with a slight chuckle. "Now I imagine she'll wear a path to Coach Clark's office."

Arlene cocked her head. "Haven't seen her make it for him. Not once."

Liz led Arlene down memory lane about past sectionals, trying to find any clue that might help. But Arlene, while competent and efficient, didn't have an eye or memory for details. After a while, Liz said goodbye and drove back to the inn, her thoughts whirling.

Why would a woman make coffee for a mouthy, self-absorbed man every day, year after year, when she wasn't required to? Arlene, though the athletic department secretary, didn't seem inclined to make coffee for anyone—in fact, she hadn't even offered Liz any.

Some women simply had been taught to take care of men. Maybe Ruth's family had fostered that notion.

But Ruth didn't fit that profile. She owned her own business. She'd been a pilot for years. She did as she pleased and said what she thought. *Subservient* was not a word that would ever describe her.

Unless it came to the basketball team. Perhaps as the über-loyal president of the booster club, she considered it her duty to support the leader of the team.

Except Arlene said Ruth hadn't made coffee for Coach Clark. Not even once.

Yet she'd done it faithfully all those years for John Albertson, as if they'd been married.

But they weren't. Instead, John had asked Kate to marry him.

Kate.

Not Ruth.

Liz caught her breath and veered her car to the side of the road, barely noticing she was downtown. Was that the factor that had detonated this whole chain of events?

Had Ruth's zeal for the booster club disguised an infatuation with John Albertson?

Impossible.

Ruth, sensible as the denim she wore. Stocky, nondescript—she'd be plain except for her snapping brown eyes. How could someone so levelheaded develop a straight-out-of-a-novel passion for Coach, with his bad haircut, big belly, and bigger mouth?

Liz lost track of time sitting in her parked car, staring at nearby half-frozen, muddy flower beds.

How unlikely that color would blossom here. Yet over time, it did.

If romance somehow had flowered for Ruth, it hadn't for Coach. He'd treated her like a pesky sister and traded barbs with her for years.

Then he'd asked Kate to marry him.

Hell hath no fury like a woman scorned.

Scattered facts, as if suddenly magnetized, lined up. Ruth owned a pharmacy. With access to all sorts of dangerous substances. She knew what would simulate a heart attack, something that, given Coach's health history and habits, would keep Dr. Sam from suspecting foul play. And coffee—everyone knew he liked it extremely strong—would disguise the taste. Especially if the poison was administered in small amounts over several weeks or months. Liz's breath congealed again. When had Coach's health worsened?

Certainly during the week before his death. But according to Asher it had begun to deteriorate earlier—about the time he'd started dating Kate.

When had the shy teacher first sensed she was being followed? *I'll bet it happened not long after Kate and John started dating.*

Liz wiped her pounding forehead. More questions, including one huge one: How did Asher and his missing status fit into this picture?

She had no idea. Perhaps Asher had unwittingly seen or heard something that threatened to expose Ruth. Maybe he'd skipped town when he heard about the burglary.

But wasn't this just more speculation on Liz's part? Truthfully, there was no proof John had been murdered; the death certificate said *heart attack.* Only one thing possibly offered a hard clue to the cause of coach's death: his coffeepot—if Ruth hadn't already dumped it and scrubbed away the evidence of her sins. Had she managed to do so before Kate and company interrupted her? *Could* she eliminate a drug's residue that easily? Or had she somehow gotten rid of the pot itself? Was the coffeepot still there?

Liz prayed for clarity of thought. Her mind replayed a video of the scene at Coach's office. When Kate opened the door, Ruth had held the coffeepot. She'd appeared more than startled. She'd wanted to take it home. Kate had grabbed the pot. Would she remember if liquid still sloshed inside it? Probably not. She wouldn't arrive home from her father's until late this evening, anyway. With Asher's safety in question, could Liz wait that long to ask her? And would questions about Coach's coffeepot send Kate off the deep end—especially if Liz's suspicions didn't pan out?

Scanning the square, Liz found the police station. She could ask Chief Houghton to test the coffeepot's contents.

But would the chief put aside the investigation of a very real burglary to focus on a theoretical poisoning connected with an incredibly theoretical love triangle? A love triangle consisting of the late Coach Albertson and two women madly in love with him, with pillar-of-the-community Ruth Bontrager so obsessed with the fat, obnoxious man that she poisoned him?

Liz imagined herself selling that notion to Chief Houghton.

Even I wouldn't believe me.

Liz exhaled in frustration. The chief certainly wouldn't allow her to examine the coffeepot on her own.

Corinne still possessed the sole key to the padlock.

Liz snorted. *As if she would hand it over to me. Even if she did, I'd be messing with a crime scene.*

Oh yes. She could picture explaining *that* to the police too.

And if the coffeepot's empty, then what? Take it and have it tested?

Not an option. A jury would consider it tainted evidence. Both she and Corinne might be suspect, and any evidence she found would be inadmissible in court without a clearly established chain of custody for the coffeepot.

However, Ruth might attempt another break-in, perhaps after consulting an expert locksmith. Or she might pay an unscrupulous one to accomplish her goal.

Liz had to protect that coffeepot, whether it was full or empty, and hide it from Ruth until Chief Houghton turned his attention from Asher's whereabouts to the office itself.

First, she had to ask Corinne for help.

I'll have to explain why. She'll think I'm crazy; she doesn't even suspect her father was murdered.

I am nuts. But do it. Now.

Liz raised her face to the fading sun in the late afternoon sky. Did she truly believe Corinne was guiltless in Coach's death?

Still arguing with herself, she got out of the car and took a brisk walk around the square, stopping briefly at an antiques shop.

Then she decided.

Liz drove purposefully back to the inn and marched upstairs.

"Here goes nothing," she said as she rapped on Corinne's door.

18

"Yes?" If anything, Corinne appeared more remote than usual. Then her gaze moved to Liz's empty hands, and her mouth drooped a little.

Great start. Liz realized she hadn't brought the usual coffee-hour hot chocolate and cookies. "I'm sorry. Hectic day. I forgot your refreshments."

"My waistline will thank you. You've spoiled me." A slight smile warmed her face. "Did you need to talk to me about something?"

Liz swallowed. "Maybe I'd better fetch the hot chocolate first. This might be an extended conversation."

"No need. I'm not thirsty." Corinne swung the door wide and pointed to an overstuffed chintz chair. "Have a seat. This chair is extra comfortable as you already know."

Liz had bought the reading chair for that very reason. She sat, pondering the irony of a guest making the innkeeper feel at home.

Corinne sat opposite her. Her tone turned businesslike. "Now, what would you like to discuss?"

Liz gulped again. How did you tell someone you thought her dad was murdered? "First, you should know I have no hard evidence. But I suspect your father's death involved foul play."

She'd expected Corinne would object vehemently. Instead, her pale face was as blank as a sheet of paper. "Go on."

"My first hint that something was wrong originated with Kate Linder."

Corinne leaned forward, as if ready to pounce.

"Yes," Liz stumbled on, "I know you dislike her. But from the start, she has insisted someone poisoned your father."

"I can believe that. She thinks I killed him." Corinne almost thrust her face into Liz's. "Do you?"

We're all alone in this house. Liz forced herself not to back away. "No, I do not."

"I-I think I believe you." Some of Corinne's rancor seemed to drain away. "What else do you need to tell me?"

Liz gripped the chair arms. "Unfortunately, your father appeared to have many enemies, but you probably know that."

"Do I ever. Some took out their hostility on my mother. She put up with it for years." Her eyes narrowed. "She would have endured anything if he'd paid even a little attention to us."

Let's not go there. Not right now. Quickly, Liz told her how she'd suspected Larry Madison, as well as Coach Clark. "I still think one of them might have had something to do with vandalism and stalking. But other suspects have appeared more likely for your father's death."

"Asher Hilty, for instance." Corinne's face hardened. "How like my dad. He poured all his time into this player and took him into his home—then the kid showed his gratitude by murdering him."

Now Liz leaned forward. "So you think he was murdered too?"

Instead of answering, Corinne crossed the room and opened the little safe provided in all the rooms. She extracted an envelope and handed it to Liz, already at her shoulder.

Heartbeat drumming a staccato in her ears, Liz stared at the smudged envelope. A letter posted from Coach to Corinne.

"Other than an occasional Christmas card, he hadn't contacted me in years." She pointed to the postmark.

Two weeks before his death.

Corinne crossed the room again to look out the window.

Liz pulled a scraggly sheet of school notebook paper from the envelope and unfolded it. Scrawled sentences, with many blots and cross outs, staggered across the page.

Dear Corinne,

I guess I should say I'm sorry I haven't been in touch. I should say I'm sorry for a lot of things. But I'd rather say them face-to-face. Soon, if I can. Life is short.

It's been tough lately. That's nothing new. Somebody has it in for me. That's nothing new either. But this feels different.

Will you meet me halfway, maybe in Kokomo?

You don't have to be nice to me. You can yell all you want. And if you don't come, I'll understand.

But I'd like to see you. I'd like it a lot.

Dad

A lot was underlined. Folding the letter, Liz closed her eyes. She didn't have to look at Corinne to know she had not met her father.

"He knew," Corinne said softly. "He knew he would die soon. Why did I pretend it was just drama? I didn't know him well, but I knew Dad wasn't that type. And 'this feels different'? Dad ignored what everyone else thought of him." A tear rolled down her cheek. "Was he talking about his bad health? Or was he trying to tell me that someone hated him enough to kill him?"

What can I say? Praying silently, Liz gently rubbed the woman's shoulder. For several minutes, she felt the tremors of Corinne's soundless grief. Then she led her to the reading chair, where the tremors diminished.

Liz said, "You don't feel like discussing this, and I don't blame you. But time may be of the essence right now, perhaps in saving an innocent life. Asher seems a likely suspect, but I have reasons to think someone else murdered your dad."

Corinne dabbed at her eyes. "I want to hear your reasons."

Liz took a deep breath. "The biggest one is that I think Ruth Bontrager was in love with your father."

Corinne's jaw dropped. "Ruth? She and my dad were friends—just friends—for decades. She knew my mom."

"That's right," Liz answered. She filled Corinne in on Ruth's devotion to her father and the possibility that she'd drugged his coffee when he decided to marry Kate instead.

She told Corinne about Kate's initial encounter with Ruth at Coach's office. "Kate grabbed the coffeepot and returned it to the office. Ruth isn't the timid type. She's bigger and stronger than Kate. This coffeepot symbolized her bond with your dad. Why didn't she insist on taking it?"

"If she'd poisoned Dad's coffee, perhaps she was afraid to draw attention to the pot." Corinne shook her head. "I can't believe she would kill him."

"I don't want to believe it either." Liz sighed, remembering Ruth's tireless support of the basketball team and her tearstained face at Coach's funeral. "In fact, I need to know I'm wrong. That's why it's important to protect the coffeepot. I think it should be tested, whether empty or full."

"Shouldn't the police do that? Wait, you haven't told them, have you?" Corinne looked at Liz as if she'd lost her mind.

"I'd like to. Right now, Chief Houghton is focused on Asher as a suspect in the burglary and possibly in your dad's death. If I asked him to test the coffeepot for poison, he'd say I was delusional. Plus, suspecting Ruth is one thing; publicly accusing her is another. I'd like to be a little more certain before I name her as a murderer. But if I'm right, Ruth will stop at nothing to get that pot. Someone has to hide it. Keep it safe in the office until it can be tested."

Corinne stared at her hands and said nothing.

Liz stayed silent too, praying the coach's daughter would help her.

Still looking down, Corinne finally spoke. "When Dad died, I should have requested an autopsy. You read his letter. He sensed something was wrong, but he didn't say he believed someone wanted to kill him. I didn't know what to think." Tears rolled down her cheeks again. "I don't want him exhumed. Not unless there's a solid reason to believe he was murdered."

Corinne stood, opened the armoire, and took out her coat and bag. "Maybe this will provide that reason. Taking two weeks off work hasn't solved anything. I haven't figured out what Dad meant in his letter. I've been afraid to enter his office or his house. I suppose I wanted to lock other people out of his life. But I locked myself out too." She shoved her arms into her coat. "I'm done with uncertainty. Let's go."

"Not right this moment," Liz cautioned, though she hated to tamper with Corinne's new resolve. "With sports and other after-school activities going on, plus janitors cleaning the school, someone's bound to ask questions before we're ready to answer. Also, I might need Mary Ann's school key—she's in and out of there during tourney time—but let's not go until eleven o'clock."

"You're right; I have a key to my dad's office and the padlock but not the front door." Corinne yanked off her coat. "Principal Oaks asked me to surrender it in exchange for the padlock key; he wanted some control over the office."

"I could use a sandwich. Want one too?" Liz didn't feel like making chatty dinner conversation, but she couldn't let Corinne think too much.

"I guess I'm a little hungry."

"I'll go pick up the key and knock on your door when I return." Liz went to her apartment and called Mary Ann. Hesitantly, she outlined her suspicions.

"*Ruth?*" Mary Ann choked as if she'd swallowed her phone. "First Larry Madison. Now you think Ruth killed John. Liz, are you crazy?"

"Yes. But this time, I think I'm right. And Corinne's willing to allow me in her dad's office, if nothing else, to eliminate Ruth as a suspect."

"She is?"

"Tonight, she is. We need to go while she's willing," Liz urged. "It's time we sought hard evidence about Coach's death. This is a start."

"I can't believe what I'm hearing. I thought better of you." Mary Ann's quiet, frozen words ripped Liz as if a fallen icicle had speared her. The silence afterward pierced her even more.

Liz clenched the phone. *Please understand. Please.* She said gently, "Think about it. Ruth loves her team, but couldn't she have used the booster club as an excuse to be near Coach every day?" Liz let her words sink in. "She had access to drugs. She had a key to the school and could have attempted to enter Coach's office to trash evidence. She knew where the cameras were located and made sure they didn't capture her on video."

"But this—this is outrageous. It can't be true." At least there was heat in Mary Ann's voice now, though it scorched Liz. "She's the best booster club president Pleasant Creek has ever had. Ruth has done everything for the team. And she would have done anything for Coach. But they were just friends. *Good* friends."

Somehow, Mary Ann's emphasis on *good* made her sound less certain.

"I can see you're not going to let this go," Mary Ann sputtered. "All right, come and get the key. But I'm only doing this because I want you proved wrong. *Wrong,* do you hear me?"

"I hope I am." Liz tried to keep the tears out of her voice. "I don't want to believe it either."

Silence again. Then, "Shouldn't you call the police so they can meet you there?"

"You know Chief Houghton thinks Asher's the problem. I'm thankful the chief is looking for him, and I don't want to pull him off the search. I don't know how his disappearance ties in, but I have a really bad feeling about it." If the police didn't find Asher soon, Liz feared the worst. And if the chief changed his focus to nabbing Ruth, he might move Asher's safety further down his priority list.

"I wish I could go with you."

Dear, fearless Mary Ann. She'd probably bring her shotgun, as she had once before. "*You* stay put and take care of that foot. Do you want Dr. Sam to ban you from the sectional?"

"I'd like to see him try," Mary Ann retorted but with less conviction than usual, so Liz knew he'd already threatened her friend with the fate she considered worse than death.

"Anyway," Liz continued, "I think Corinne might feel more comfortable if only I accompanied her."

"You're probably right." Mary Ann exhaled. "I hate it when you're right. But I still think you're wrong. Anyway . . . come and pick up the key. Come before I change my mind."

When Mary Ann met her on the front porch, Liz could hardly look at her stricken face, with its crooked, grieving mouth.

"It fits only the north entrance, but that's the one closest to Coach's office." Mary Ann handed her the key, then hugged Liz so hard she could barely breathe. "Be careful. Someone chased you too, remember? Call me when you're done there."

"We're not going until eleven and will stay only a few minutes. I hate to wake you."

"I won't go to bed until I hear from you, and if it's not by eleven thirty I'm calling the police. I'm on pain medicine and might fall asleep, so let it ring."

Yes, Mother. Her own mother had annoyed her with that "call me" request so many times. But tonight, Liz savored it.

On the way home, she glanced at the rearview mirror so often, she nearly ran a stop sign. The welcoming lights she'd turned on earlier warmed her fears away as she turned into the inn's driveway.

Corinne's shy smile, almost like a teen's, greeted her at the front door. The kitchen's homey atmosphere eased Liz's remaining tensions. As they slapped together turkey-avocado wraps and heated leftover chicken noodle soup, Liz could almost see Corinne as a girlfriend who'd come over to share supper. Watching a movie together slowed her heart rate and almost pushed their errand to the back of her mind.

Almost.

When the mantel clock struck ten, Liz packed a large tote with pepper spray, a flashlight, and other items they might need. "I'm getting antsy. Let's go out for dessert."

"Okay." Corinne shot her a dubious glance. "Is anyplace open around here?"

Liz chuckled. "Only Burger Heaven out by the interstate. It's not far from the school, and I've heard they have good sundaes and fried apple pies. Everyone needs a dose of junk food from time to time. I think this is a two-pie night."

Only a few travelers were in the restaurant when they arrived. Noisy teens, a tired-looking trucker, and two wide-awake children with a mother who looked downright exhausted.

In low tones, Liz and Corinne discussed specifics about their visit to Coach's office.

Liz said, "If the coffeepot is there, where will we hide it?"

Corinne's nose wrinkled. "I only looked inside the office once, that day you were there. I don't know how Dad found anything in that mess."

"Ruth found her booster club files. She spent a lot of time there, so she probably knows it better than almost anyone." Liz frowned. "Maybe every nook and cranny."

"Except . . ." Corinne paused.

"Except what?"

"Except for a little cabinet-like space in the back of his desk against the wall. It had a false front, and Dad kept his basketball signed by Larry Bird there. Bird signed it in 1979, the year Indiana State—Dad's alma mater—played in the national championship. I guess Dad wanted to keep it near but didn't want to risk it being stolen."

Corinne's face softened. "When I was four, he opened the cabinet and showed it to me. He told me not to tell anyone about it; the ball and its hiding place were our special secret." Her eyes moistened. "And I haven't—until now."

Liz stirred her coffee, letting the other woman relive the poignant daddy/daughter moment.

Corinne found her way back to the present. "I think it's the same desk. Maybe that will be our hiding place."

"Sounds like the best bet." Hopefully, John Albertson had never confided in Ruth about his beloved basketball's secret location.

Corinne wiped her eyes with a tissue.

Liz patted her arm and turned her attention to the parking lot to give her friend time to recover her composure.

After they'd finished eating, they hopped into Liz's Acura and sped toward the high school. Corinne leaned forward as if that would help them reach it sooner. Anxiety coiled in Liz as well.

Liz's pulse thudded in her chest as she parked at the north entrance. Between sugar, caffeine, and tension, Liz and Corinne shot out of the car as if they had been ejected.

Liz took the pepper spray from her bag and pulled on gloves. She shone her tiny but powerful flashlight on the door and unlocked it. As it clanged shut, dim lights greeted them. Their footsteps echoed in the shadowy, waxy-smelling halls. Corinne, also wearing gloves, unlocked the padlock on her father's office door. As it opened, its *clink* resounded like broken bells.

Corinne removed the padlock, then inserted the key into the lock. They entered, and the gym-shoe smell withered Liz's nostrils. Even as Corinne flipped on the light, Liz spotted the black handle of the squat metal coffeepot, still sitting on its hot plate, as if waiting to serve Coach. She shook the coffeepot gently.

Slosh.

"Yes," Liz whispered, pumping her fist. She locked the office door from the inside. "Now, could you show me the hiding place?"

Corinne stared at the coffeepot as if she'd never seen one. Her head swiveled in slow motion as she gazed around the chaotic office, perhaps hoping her dad would appear.

Liz slipped an arm around her shoulders. "I know this is very hard for you. I'll come back with you later to sort through his office, but we need to hide the coffeepot. Right now."

Corinne shook her head as if waking from a trance. She matched Liz's whisper. "Of course. I'm sorry."

Liz pushed the big, awkward chair aside, and Corinne dropped to her knees, reaching inside the cubbyhole. Her muffled voice alternated with scraping sounds. "Found it . . . having a harder time opening it than Dad did."

Please hurry. But she knew Corinne was working as fast as she could. While Liz waited she searched for alternative hiding spots.

"Got it!" Corinne backed out of the cubbyhole, her cheeks flushed, clutching an old basketball. She stared at its signature, obviously consumed with the past.

Liz handed Corinne her cell phone, ready to video. "Film me moving the pot." At Corinne's nod, Liz picked up the pot and rounded the desk, explaining what she was doing and why and keeping the coffeepot in the frame at all times. Liz sank to her knees and stuck it inside the small cabinet, sliding its false front in place.

She discreetly sealed the panel with a piece of clear tape. If only it could be locked away. But the hiding place was well disguised, and she hoped it wouldn't be needed for long. She got out of the cubbyhole, heartbeat thundering in triumph, and stood. "Mission accomplished. Let's go."

Corinne ended the video and handed the phone back to her. Liz emailed it to herself and Mary Ann, confident the other woman wouldn't check her emails before morning. Corinne stowed the ball inside a dust-covered case of old trophies. Liz unlocked the door, cracked it, and listened. Corinne raised her head like a startled deer.

Only the school's heating system hummed, with a few small echoes of nighttime building sounds, like ripples in a stream.

Their eyes met. *Go for it.*

Grasping her can of pepper spray, Liz slowly opened the door and peered into the hallway.

No one.

They slipped out, and Corinne locked the door. Liz readied the padlock.

Someone laughed.

Liz whipped around. Ruth laughed again, brash and friendly as if they were late for a quilting party.

She was pointing a gun.

19

"Where were you hiding?" Liz blurted.

"First things first," Ruth said cheerily. "Drop the pepper spray. Roll the can toward me with your foot."

Given her distance from them, the spray was useless. Though Liz wanted to throw it at Ruth, she complied.

"Now, on to more important matters." Ruth wiggled the gun slightly toward Corinne. "Unlock that door again. Then get me my coffeepot."

Liz tried to feign confusion. The less Ruth thought they knew, the better their chance of survival, right?

"Don't pretend you don't know what's going on." Ruth laughed scornfully. "Did you really think I wouldn't find out how you pumped Arlene about my coffee-brewing skills? Get the pot, Corinne. Now."

"It was my father's, not yours." She glared at Ruth.

"Corinne, she has a gun." Liz kept her voice even. "Open the door. Give it to her."

"Very sensible advice. I'd take it, if I were you." The faux cordial tone continued, but Liz easily detected its sneer. "To clarify matters, I brought my old coffeepot to the office years ago. It has always belonged to me."

But Coach never belonged to you, did he? Liz bit her tongue to keep from saying it.

Corinne opened the office door, then retrieved the coffeepot and gave it to Ruth.

"Good girl." She grasped it and demanded they relock and re-padlock the door. "Why worry Arlene when you don't have to?" She ordered them to turn off their phones and hand them over.

"How did you know we'd come tonight?" Corinne ground the words between her teeth.

"Actually, I didn't. I thought I would have to fiddle with that blasted padlock again. But you showed up just in time to help me. I appreciate that so much."

"You've been stalking me?" Liz tried to keep her talking. *Might buy us some time.*

"Only because you got nosy. We're friendly here in the Midwest, but we mind our own business."

"Even if your business is murder? I don't think so," Corinne spat. "You poisoned my father!"

Silence. Ruth marched them down the hall.

Cold wind blasted the trio as they exited the school.

Liz demanded, "Where have you hidden Asher?"

"My, aren't you the smart ones. You'll know soon enough." No trace of a chuckle now. "Turn to the right. Walk around the building to the van."

Her tone raised the hair on Liz's neck. But small delays might add up to someone seeing their predicament. She followed Corinne slowly to an older, dark cargo van parked behind a Dumpster. Its license plate had been covered.

Ruth wasn't taking any chances that they'd memorize the number. Their captor's cunning chipped away at Liz's waning optimism.

Still, Mary Ann's expecting us to call.

But had she stayed awake?

"Stop." Training the gun on them, Ruth opened the passenger door and placed the coffeepot in a box on the floor. "Don't want Houghton to find this in the trash, do we? I won't even pour it out yet. Don't want this anywhere on the school grounds. No, I'll find a better place to ditch it; once we leave here, it's just another coffeepot."

Ruth handed Liz a roll of duct tape from her coat pocket. "Slap a strip across Corinne's mouth, nice and tight, and tie her wrists behind her."

Liz had come to treasure duct tape for little repairs at the inn, but now she battled its stickiness.

"I've sold you duct tape," Ruth barked, "so don't act like you've never seen it before."

Liz stopped fumbling. "Yes, I was your customer and your friend, Ruth."

The cold barrel of the handgun jabbed her temple. "Just do what I tell you."

Liz finished her task, hating the fear and fury in Corinne's eyes as she bound her.

Don't give up. There are two of us and only one of her.

Ruth ordered both into the seatless back of the van.

Wonderful. Tossed into a van again. Hadn't she done this drill not two months ago? This had never happened in Boston, not once in forty years.

Ruth forced Liz to tape Corinne's ankles and then her own. Their kidnapper mashed a strip over Liz's lips. "Put your hands behind your back. Don't move. Don't even take a deep breath, you hear me? Or I might think you're trying something."

Liz wanted to bare her teeth, but tape covered her mouth.

After checking their bonds, Ruth slammed the door, walked around the van's rear, and took her place in the driver's seat.

She'd probably removed the cover from the license plate to avoid arousing suspicion. Why hadn't she blindfolded them? Even with no windows, they might pick up details of where she was taking them.

But that won't matter if we don't live to tell anyone, will it?

Bile rose in Liz's throat.

Ruth's turn out of the school parking lot threw both women to the floor.

Liz's head and nauseous stomach absorbed every bump. The engine's heat under the gritty floor fried one cheek. Corinne's head and torso rested on top of her. Liz tried to shift her head, but she couldn't move. *Lord, please help us. Help Asher, wherever he is.*

Ruth's turn told her, not surprisingly, that they were headed away from Pleasant Creek. They'd encounter no towns for at least fifteen miles. Soon she lost any sense of direction as the van meandered along back roads. Liz tried to remember details that would identify their surroundings, but she faced away from the front windows. The van traveled at moderate speed. No entrance ramps or interstate traffic. At one point, a train rumbled beside them. A confused rooster crowed twice in the night.

Meanwhile, Corinne attempted to wrestle herself off Liz. At one point, her fingers patted Liz's back. *It will be all right.*

Corinne hadn't given up either. And now, Liz could turn her head. A small candle of hope lit the gloom in the back of the van.

Head movement mostly gave her a better view of the back of Ruth's head. *Not what I want to see.* But she detected some trees through the front and passenger windows. An occasional house. Liz estimated they'd been traveling half an hour when the van lurched to a stop. Ruth exited the van and flung the contents of the coffeepot into a field.

Liz and Corinne exchanged worried glances, wondering when this madness would end. After another ten minutes of driving Ruth again came to a halt, and this time, she stopped the engine.

Liz's queasy stomach shouted hurrahs. Her mind, not so much. But she struggled to a half-sitting position and took in what she could. A large building loomed some distance away, barely lit by surrounding lights. A barn? It didn't strike her that way.

Was Asher in there? *Dead or alive?*

She smashed that thought.

Ruth can't carry us inside. If she wants us there, she'll have to free our ankles.

Could they kick, slowing her plans? Hurt her enough to make her drop her gun?

Perhaps Liz could distract Ruth with an attempt to run for it, leaving Corinne free to escape and get help.

If only she could talk to Corinne—

Ruth hauled the squeaky doors open. "End of the line? Maybe."

She pulled something from her bag. The lights gleamed on the blades of a large pair of scissors.

Liz readied her feet to attack. She sensed Corinne stiffening too.

"Now, don't get uptight, girls," Ruth cautioned, a smile still coloring her voice. "I'm just releasing your feet." She removed something else from the bag. "As long as you cooperate."

She pointed the gun at them again.

We can't fight her lying down. Liz controlled the urge to kick while Ruth cut the tape that bound her ankles. Then she cut Corinne's tape.

Ruth yanked on Liz's leg. "Come on, slide out of there. You can do it. You, too, sweetie."

At the childhood term of endearment, Corinne let loose a low growl.

Chill, Corinne. Show your anger and she'll enjoy this more.

Her fellow captive quieted, as if she realized it too.

What was this place?

After her eyes adjusted to the night, Liz knew: an airport. Certainly not a major one, as Ruth wouldn't allow them to be seen in the open like this. There were two hangars, a couple of small planes sitting alongside them in the shadows, and a smaller building. All deserted.

"Call me a softie"—Ruth ripped the tape from their mouths—"but I really don't like gagging people."

Liz fought off a scream.

"Yell all you want." Ruth waved her free hand at the dark, endless fields that surrounded the airport. "Nobody's gonna hear you. Not this time of night."

"Where are we?" Corinne demanded.

"Let's just say we're between three towns that roll up their sidewalks at night like this airport does." Taking the box with the now-empty coffeepot from the passenger side, she pointed with the gun toward the nearest hangar. As Liz and Corinne trudged along, Ruth followed, yakking. "Not much wind. Few clouds. Nice night for flying, don't you think?"

Liz's blood ran cold. "Where are you taking us?"

"Cabin where my family and I spent vacations in Kentucky, right across the Ohio River. A little cold this time of year, but you won't mind that."

Because you'll kill us. Now? Later? Liz's bound hands clenched. Dead or alive, they wouldn't be found for days. But in case they survived this mess, Liz wanted to milk their kidnapper for all she could. "Is that where you took Asher?"

"Maybe."

"Why? What did he do to you?"

"I wouldn't have bothered with that half-wit if he hadn't opened his big mouth. At Mama's, remember? I sat in the booth behind you while he told you all about John's going downhill. About his episodes of confusion."

Ruth *had* greeted them in the restaurant—the only "friendly" person who didn't ignore Asher. Horror squeezed Liz's throat.

"I didn't want to go after Asher." Ruth's smug tone raked Liz's nerves. "Actually, he was rather convenient. Everyone blamed him for everything. Houghton certainly did."

At times, I did. Liz gritted her teeth.

"Living with John, he saw too much and remembered too well. You listened to him when no one else did, Liz. I couldn't let you ask any more questions."

They were passing the planes next to the hangar. *Better make a break for it soon.* If she could dash behind the nearest one—

"Don't even think about it." Ruth thrust the gun into Liz's temple, and her tone turned deadly. "I've heard about stuff you've pulled in the past. No way will you do it now. Move before I lose patience."

With the gun still aimed at them, Ruth put down the box and unlocked the hangar's side door. Seething, Liz followed Corinne into the cavernous building that reeked of oil and grease. Dim light outlined two small planes.

Ruth entered behind her. Facing Liz and Corinne, she backed toward the nearest one, opened its cockpit, and pushed the all-important box inside. She patted the plane's wing. "Girls, meet *Amazon*. I named her that before any company started selling books online. I always liked those stories about strong women—strong women like me."

Liz longed to smack Ruth in the mouth, but with bound hands, the only weapon she could wield was her own mouth. "I must say I underestimated you."

"Most people do. They think they know me. But they have no idea what I can do." The woman practically purred.

Liz decided to try a different tactic. "They believe a woman who doesn't look like an airbrushed bimbo is worthless."

"Isn't that the truth?" For a moment, Ruth seemed lost in thought. "Why don't they get it? Why can't they see that a smart, strong woman is what they need?"

Apparently feeding off Liz's vibes, Corinne said, "I'll never understand what Dad saw in Kate."

Ruth poisoned the air with a stream of expletives. Like a caged predator, she began to pace.

Corinne, watch me. Slowly, Liz turned halfway toward Ruth.

Corinne, catching Liz's glance, followed her lead as Ruth's rage escalated.

"Skinny, helpless, stupid little witch!" Ruth's face contorted. "It's like she cast a spell on John. She had nothing in common with him."

"I'm not sure she knows anything about basketball." Liz gestured toward their captor with a slight dip of her head. She sensed Corinne watching her as she softly tapped the floor with a foot. *One.*

"She tried to fake it. He knew that. He even *liked* it!" Ruth snarled like an animal. "I did everything for John. I deserved him. She didn't!"

Liz tapped again. *Two.*

Ruth's tears splattered the grimy cement floor as her rage bubbled over. She kicked the plane's tires. "Why couldn't she have left him alone? She *made* me kill John! Why, why . . . ?"

Three.

Liz charged. Corinne attacked. Their combined force slammed Ruth to the floor.

Kick her! Dislodge the gun!

Ruth rammed the weapon into Corinne's neck even as the other woman lay on top of her. "Good try, girls. But make another move like that and she dies."

20

Corinne jabbed Liz in the side with her elbow.

Forget it, Corinne. I won't fight her. Liz's body had shut down. Her arms, still bound like sticks behind her back, had numbed to uselessness.

They'd had their chance. Would they get another? *Mary Ann, did you fall asleep waiting for us to call?*

"Get off me." Still holding Corinne at gunpoint, Ruth cursed and kicked at them.

Liz smothered her moan and slid away.

"Stand up, both of you. Stand still. Real still." She moved sideways toward the plane. Facing them, she threw open the door.

As Liz stumbled to her feet, a flame of anger that licked at her insides billowed into wildfire. "Do you think no one will notice we're missing?"

"Oh, they will." Ruth's friendly arrogance returned. "But you'll be long gone before they realize it. So will I. Not the same place, of course. I'm going somewhere warm." She stretched, as if imagining lying on a beach. "Perhaps a tropical paradise, run by people who mind their own business—for a price."

Liz snorted. "That could get expensive, don't you think?"

"I'm not worried about money." She winked, as if they shared a secret, then sighed. "But I missed a game tonight. And I'll miss the sectional games. I hate that. The team will be fired up. They could win this year."

"I can't believe you," Corinne spat. "You're worried about winning some stupid basketball games?"

Got to shake her. Liz shouted, "Kate will go to the games. You won't. Though you loved John, you killed him. But Kate still lives."

A brutal slap knocked Liz to the floor. "Not for long," Ruth shrieked. "Just because I'll be out of the country doesn't mean she's out of my reach. Oh, what I have planned for her. I'll tell you all about it on the way—"

A child-size blur slammed into Ruth from behind.

Kate.

Liz tensed, ready to spring. But this "helpless" Kate didn't need Liz's assistance. Her punches pummeled Ruth's head and chest. The gun flew from the older woman's fingers, spinning on the floor close to Corinne. Hands still bound, she booted the gun to the other side of the hangar.

Liz darted to the plane's metal propeller, turned, and rubbed her duct tape shackles against its edge. Corinne soon joined her, and they worked on their bonds together as their petite rescuer wove in and out, landing blow after blow on her bigger, stronger opponent. Ruth roared like a wounded lioness, charging and grabbing at Kate as if she would tear her to pieces.

Liz rubbed harder, faster, praying she'd get to Kate in time to help. But Sadie suddenly appeared, pointing a .22 at the fighters, and now joy, rather than desperation, fueled her attempts. *Oh, thank you, God. Thank you.*

Naomi dashed from the shadows, pulling scissors from Sadie's bag to finish cutting the tape. All three ran to Sadie, still watching the two duke it out.

"Should we do something?" Corinne said.

"Kate wanted to handle this." Sadie's normally sparkly eyes had narrowed to slits. "But I'll be on Ruth like ugly on an ape if she gets the drop on Kate."

"So will I." Naomi's dark eyes glowed like blazing coals.

Let's take turns.

Kate was doing fine by herself, thank you very much. So well that Liz wondered if they should intervene. "Sadie, don't you think—?"

Kate's foot connected with Ruth's mouth, and the larger woman finally toppled to the floor. Kate stood over her, panting, sweat dripping from her twisted face. "You thought you'd kill me too? Only in your dreams." She kicked Ruth's inert body.

Naomi edged between Kate and her fallen enemy. "It's over, dear." Slipping an arm around her, Naomi tugged her away from Ruth.

Corinne knelt and, with a look of extreme distaste, checked Ruth's pulse. "Still strong, though she's not moving much."

Liz hugged Kate. "I hate to think of what would have happened if you hadn't come. Oh, my word, I had no idea you could do that."

"I didn't either. A little different from the classes." She stumbled farther away from Ruth and dropped to the floor.

This time, we're tying your *hands.* Liz pulled the duct tape from Ruth's coat pockets. Corinne helped her bind their ex-captor. But even with a second search of her pockets, Liz didn't find their phones. "Naomi, may I use your cell? Ruth took ours."

"The police are already on their way." Sadie moved closer and aimed her gun at Ruth. "Mary Ann called them after she called us."

Liz gasped, "How did you know where to find us?"

"We wouldn't have, except when we were approaching the school, we saw Ruth pull out of the parking lot." Sadie loosened her grip on her gun and squeezed Liz's hand, then grasped her weapon again. "We had to stay a ways back. Once we figured you were going to the airport, I took a different road or two so she wouldn't see us."

"Saved by the cavalry," Liz said lightly, but her eyes teared.

"Opal and Caitlyn should be here soon too." Sadie clucked her tongue. "Hopefully, they've talked Mary Ann into staying home, where she belongs."

"We did. Just barely." The other Material Girls hurried in, gaping at Ruth's still form.

"Thank God you're all right," Opal said.

"Thank God you all came." Sweet relief dripped through Liz,

then flowed like a brook after a spring rain. She, Sadie, Opal, and Caitlyn joined Naomi and a still-panting Kate in a silent, minute-long group hug.

A separate, longing gaze nearby drew her eye. Liz gently disengaged herself from the group, turned, and threw her arms around Corinne.

————— /////////////////////// —————

"How many lives do you have left, Liz?" Chief Houghton shook his head. "If you had nine when you moved here, I think you're down to five by now."

"You might be right." Now that the immediate crisis had passed, Liz's knees had turned to water. She sank to the hangar floor, suddenly realizing she was sitting with Kate on one side and Corinne on the other.

"If Ruth has only one, she sure messed it up." Sadness filled the police chief's face as he talked to an area sheriff and directed Officer Dixon to take her, now awake, to his squad car.

Liz's own bumps and bruises couldn't compare to Ruth's. How did the booster club president walk after that beating? Nevertheless, the silent woman's eyes burned like two vicious flames. Her mouth worked as she and the officer passed.

Is she going to spit on Kate? Both Liz and Naomi moved to protect her.

Dixon hurried Ruth away.

"I thought she was a good woman in many ways. She had lots of friends," Chief Houghton said. "Why did she let this go so far?"

Who knows? Liz looked around at the other Material Girls and at Kate and Corinne. A moment ago, it had been enough that they stopped Ruth. That they were safe. But now . . . "Please let us know when you find Asher."

"I imagine that kid has nine lives too." Houghton frowned. "We're contacting Ruth's relatives to locate the cabin. The sheriff is on the line with the Kentucky State Police right now."

He glanced at Ruth's box containing the empty coffeepot. "To think that thing played such a big role in all this. Even I knew Ruth made coffee for Coach every day—though I couldn't tell you why. She'd done it so long, nobody thought a thing about it. I only wish we had some of the coffee left to send to a lab. Fingerprints won't do any good since she touched it so often."

"But, Chief," Liz said, "this isn't Coach's coffeepot."

"It's not?" He stared at her, then at the box, as if it were bewitched.

"Liz Eckardt, you *are* crazy," Sadie shrieked, and the others gaped.

"No, I'm not." She and Corinne exchanged glances. "This is a decoy pot. The real thing is safe and sound back at Coach's office—with quite a bit of old coffee waiting for the lab."

———— *///////////////////////* ————

"He acts like he's still mad," Sadie said as Chief Houghton, shoulders stiff with disapproval, strode out of the hangar, headed for the school. "Guess he didn't like your setting a trap for Ruth or your little movie."

"You did take terrible risks." Opal gave Liz and Corinne a stern look.

Liz sighed. "It wasn't really a trap."

"It wasn't?" Naomi snorted. "You knew Ruth would find out about your chat with Arlene. You bought the fake pot at an antique store. You poured coffee into it and set it on the burner in Coach's office."

"Hey, Corinne helped me plan this." Liz wasn't going to take all the credit or the blame for their scheme.

"It was a trap, pure and simple." For the first time that evening, Corinne smiled. "And when we handed Ruth that decoy pot, she took the bait, didn't she?"

"Boy, did she ever," Caitlyn crowed.

Opal applauded.

"In a way, I hoped she wouldn't come tonight," Liz admitted.

"I could have done without being hog-tied." Corinne grimaced.

"Me too." Liz wearily rubbed still-tense lines from her forehead. "We did have a Plan B. If Ruth hadn't come tonight, we would have left the decoy pot on the burner, hoping she'd soon be caught trying to steal it. Then I would have told the chief someone had taken the decoy and urged him to have the real pot tested immediately. But any delay might have meant Asher's death." Her eyes teared, though they'd learned he was safe. "Sometimes you have to take a risk or two."

The others murmured with admiration and reproach.

"We plotted together while we were eating fried pies out at Burger Heaven," Corinne added. "I'll never forget how Liz looked, munching away, looking so wholesome and harmless, as if she wouldn't hurt a fly. Ha!"

"Kate's scary too," Naomi declared. "Next time we go to a movie, I'm letting her pick. No arguments."

Actually this whole group is pretty dangerous, Liz concluded, *though we don't look it right now.*

Huddled together, sitting on the floor of the hangar, they mostly looked exhausted.

Liz checked her phone, now back in her possession. Past one o'clock in the morning.

They'd celebrate soon enough, but right now, they needed to go home. If only she could get her legs to move.

Corinne stirred beside her. Half her perfect chignon hung down her back, and the hair around her face had actually dared to frizz. The coach's daughter brushed messy dark tendrils from her eyes, then looked at Kate.

Kate stared back.

Liz couldn't help cringing. *Am I in the line of fire again?*

"Thank you." Corinne's tone sounded wooden, but her words didn't. "Thank you for saving my life."

21

"**M**aybe I'd better eat your bacon." Sadie reached for Mary Ann's plate. "Today being a sectional game day, you don't want grease all over your cheerleader getup, do you?"

Mary Ann yanked her plate away. "You don't want to lose your fingers, do you?"

Since Liz's returning guests had met friends at Mama's for a pregame lunch, she'd invited the Material Girls to a celebratory brunch at the inn where they could hash out all their questions over bacon, an egg-and-four-cheese casserole, fruit, and Naomi's homemade cinnamon rolls.

For now, they delayed any serious discussion in order to lay bets on who would win the bacon battle.

The past couple of weeks, they'd all trudged through tensions as thick as March mud, but today Liz practically danced to the kitchen to fetch more bacon. She returned to the dining room and set the heaping platter on the table. "Sorry to spoil the fight, but I made enough to feed the whole basketball team."

"I guess I don't mind that *too* much." Sadie piled a few forkfuls onto her plate.

"As if you didn't eat enough at the spaghetti supper last night," Mary Ann teased. "You set the school record for refills."

Liz was thankful that Kiera joined in the group's feasting and bantering, but she wished Corinne and Kate had come. Corinne had said she might, but her door remained closed. She had, however, begun cleaning out Coach's office and home. That was a good start. Perhaps talking openly about her dad's death to a group—even this caring bunch—might prove more than she could process right now.

Kate said flat out that she couldn't handle it; she wasn't coming. Nor had she made up her mind whether to attend the sectional games.

"Kate relived John's death all over again when Ruth confessed everything." Naomi pushed back her plate. "She couldn't believe anyone could hate John enough to kill him, and the fact that their happiness was the catalyst for his death really twisted the knife."

Kiera paused in chewing a large cinnamon roll. "Wasn't Ms. Bontrager supposed to be, like, in love with Coach?" Her expression said plainly that even if old people could fall in love, Ruth and Coach were the least likely candidates in the world.

Ordinarily, Liz would hide a grin. But she said soberly, "Either she wasn't really in love with him—"

"She wasn't," Mary Ann sniffed, battering rather than buttering her toast.

"—or she let her love turn to obsession. Supposedly, there's a thin line between love and hate." Liz shrugged. "At any rate, she'd decided Coach was hers and no other woman could have him."

"But that's stupid. Why go to prison your whole life because of some ugly old guy like Coach?"

Maybe it's a good thing neither Kate nor Corinne came. Ignoring Kiera's dig, Liz continued, "Coach Albertson's murder may or may not have been a crime of passion, but Ruth had another big reason for drugging his coffee with Thorazine."

"What reason?" Now Naomi, Opal, and Caitlyn, like Kiera, were sitting on the edge of their chairs.

"Mary Ann, Sadie, and I helped Corinne and the police go through some of Coach's files, both paper and computer." Liz shook her head. "How I wish we'd done it sooner, but no one suspected . . . He'd found evidence Ruth had stolen booster club funds. For decades!"

"What?" Forks halted throughout the room.

"When she was holding us in the hangar, she hinted at having money," Liz said. "It didn't occur to me that she'd pocketed a large percentage of the funds she'd helped raise. But then we found proof she'd been embezzling from the club."

Opal looked dazed. "What did you find in Coach's office?"

"He copied pages from Ruth's ledger," Liz explained. "I don't know what triggered his suspicions, but he'd circled amounts that didn't make sense, scanned pages, and hid them in computer files. It's unclear why he didn't turn Ruth in; Corinne thinks he wanted to give her a chance to confess."

"That's why we think he confronted Ruth." Sadie snorted in disgust. "Not a bright thing to do."

"How do you know?" Kiera's inquisitive eyes peered over her mug of hot chocolate. "Did somebody hear them fight?"

"Not as far as we know. But I found something in his journal—though he mostly recorded basketball stuff." Sadie cringed. "Three days before he died, John wrote that they met. Five words: 'Talked to Ruth. Not good.' He was generous, giving her time to turn herself in. Always did treat her like his sister."

"We found no evidence that he knew she'd been drugging his coffee," Liz added. "Maybe he really believed she'd do the right thing."

Sadie harrumphed, "Fat chance."

Liz turned to Kiera. "Actually, Ruth admitted to nearly everything once the chief confronted her with Coach's record of her embezzlement. I'm not sure why she could lie so boldly for so long and then just completely fall apart and confess everything over proof of her stealing, especially when she stayed mum after committing murder and kidnapping Asher and us."

"She probably recalled the moment when Coach told her he knew about her theft," Caitlyn suggested. "I bet he didn't sugarcoat it."

"Probably called her a thief and a few other things." Sadie rapped the table. "And she deserved it!"

"Still hard to hear someone you love tear you to pieces," Opal said sadly. "Until then, Ruth might have been able to lie to herself about slipping small amounts of Thorazine into his coffee, pilfering money—"

"—telling herself she was only playing pranks by slashing tires, writing nasty letters, and throwing bricks," Liz went on. "According to the chief, Ruth claimed she was 'just trying to scare' me when she chased me around the lake—as if we were playing a game."

"Some game." Sadie crossed her arms.

"When Coach threatened to expose Ruth, there was no turning back." Liz paused. *If only she had. Things would have worked out better, even for Ruth. For everyone . . .*

Liz continued, "That Monday, Ruth made coffee for him, as usual. Arlene said she would brew it even when they fought. Only this time Ruth added a big dose of Thorazine. Students were absent because teachers were at an off-campus training session, Arlene had taken a personal day, knowing there wouldn't be much to do. It's possible that's when Coach chose to confront Ruth about her illegal activities, wanting to do so quietly. Regardless, no one was there to help when Coach's systems began to shut down."

"How I wish *Ruth* had asked for help." At the grief in Mary Ann's tone, everyone fell silent. She toyed with the cinnamon roll on her plate, then pushed it away. "If I'd known her drugstore was struggling, I would have done what I could. Other friends would have pitched in. Or the bank might have worked something out." Her face darkened, and she thumped her coffee mug. "But no. She had to steal from all of us. From the whole town, even at Coach's funeral."

"At the start, maybe Ruth didn't intend to do anything wrong." Opal's gentle voice intervened. "She probably borrowed a little when she was strapped, paying it back when she could. I remember both her parents were sick for a long time."

"I imagine big discount stores and mail-order pharmacies have been taking her business these past several years too," Caitlyn said. "Maybe she thought she had to steal to stay open."

"That's exactly what she told Chief Houghton." Though her own sympathy for Ruth remained minimal, Liz appreciated their positive slants. No one wanted a hate fest. "Dosing Coach with Thorazine started small too. The pathologist who examined his exhumed body said he'd taken in small amounts of the drug for approximately three months before Ruth gave him the final large dose."

"So she started putting it in his coffee in November?" Naomi's gaze hardened. "About the time Coach and Kate started dating."

Liz nodded. "Ruth admitted she'd hoped Kate was just a fling. But when it continued, Ruth felt she had to do something."

"How did she get away with it?" Kiera looked from Liz to Naomi to the others. "Wouldn't Coach have tasted the Thor—Thor—whatever that was?"

Liz answered, "Everyone knew Coach liked his coffee extra strong—which hid the taste."

"Do you think, in giving those weak doses of Thorazine, she was delivering some sort of warning to Coach?" Sadie's brows bunched.

"Maybe. I think she mostly wanted to make him miserable," Caitlyn answered. "She wanted revenge."

Liz nodded at the nurse. "Dr. Sam told Chief Houghton she picked the perfect drug to do exactly that. The doc used to prescribe Thorazine for some mental illnesses. But he switched to newer medicines because Thorazine caused too many side effects."

"I've seen those side effects when taking care of a few patients on Thorazine. Weakness, dizziness, and the confusion Coach suffered," Caitlyn affirmed. "Being a pharmacist, Ruth knew that."

"But I heard the state cracked down on prescription-drug use," Opal protested. "Owner or not, wouldn't someone have nailed Ruth for dipping into the pharmacy's drug supply?"

Caitlyn nodded. "If she'd given Coach a newer, more commonly used drug. Thorazine's still found in pharmacies, especially in rural areas. But it's not on the list of drugs monitored so carefully by the state. Plus, she didn't use a large amount until that last dose. Easy to disguise records when small quantities are involved."

"Paired with Coach's previous heart problems, the large dose's effect resembled a fatal heart attack." Liz glanced at Mary Ann. "The pathologist said no doctor could have detected the drug without the lab tests that accompany an autopsy."

At her friend's smile, Liz gave an inward sigh of relief. *She's convinced I wasn't knocking Dr. Sam or his diagnosis. Finally.*

Sadie moaned. "It scares me that I kind of understand Ruth's logic. She wouldn't shoot Coach, but she sure tried to keep him feeling miserable. Then he wouldn't go out with Kate, or Kate would think twice about dating a sick, older man."

"Didn't work," Naomi said. "He was head over heels in love with Kate, and she with him."

"Why didn't Ms. Bontrager murder Ms. Linder instead?" Kiera inquired. "Why kill the guy she wanted to marry?"

"Great questions," Liz responded. "Questions I've asked too. But I doubt Ruth will tell us all her motivations; she probably doesn't even understand them herself. My guess? This is a small town. Shooting or knifing a person would create enormous risks of being seen. Too many people here keep track of friends and neighbors—like Naomi." Liz patted her friend's hand. "You stuck with Kate. You probably saved her life."

The others murmured agreement. Naomi's cheeks reddened, but her eyes shone.

Remembering her own impatience with Coach's fiancée, Liz raised a silent prayer. *God, please help me be a friend like Naomi.*

Liz went on, "Ruth didn't know Kate personally or have the opportunity to poison her, as she did Coach Albertson. So she stuck to stalking and vandalizing, which she hoped would intimidate Kate. But I don't think Ruth had decided to live and let live. She assured Corinne and me that Kate wasn't beyond her reach. By then she'd lost all sense of right and wrong." She shuddered. "Thank God we were rescued before Ruth could carry out the rest of her nasty plans."

"And thank God you caught on." Opal joined in the group shiver. "The rest of us were blind to her obsession with John Albertson."

"I didn't have a clue until I remembered seeing Ruth holding that pot and asked myself: Would I make coffee for a man every day for decades for no reason?"

Kiera sniffed. "My husband had better make it for *me*."

The room echoed with laughter.

Thank you, Kiera. We needed that.

Amid the chuckles, a tall figure filled the doorway. "Um . . . am I interrupting something?"

22

More giggles erupted as Asher glanced around, looking bewildered.

Liz experienced a pang of wistfulness that overwhelmed her mirth. Asher reminded her of Steve in so many ways.

Sadie hugged him. "Sit down and eat, boy." She started piling food on a plate for him.

When he plopped beside Kiera, the teen girl's eyes sparkled. But she didn't look inclined to pour him any coffee.

They allowed Asher to chow down while they discussed the weather and other important concerns, but Liz knew they ached to hear his side of the story. Chief Houghton had been stingy with details.

Liz surveyed the group's bright, inquiring eyes. She'd warned Asher beforehand—and he'd still come. As the boy finished off three platefuls, she wondered if Asher really knew what he was in for. "You're a brave guy to eat with a bunch of scary women."

"I've met scary women before. You guys aren't so bad." Though his tone was light, he set his jaw. "I s'pose you all want to know about my little side trip to Kentucky."

Silence.

If only you knew how rare that *is.* Liz sensed ears perking up.

"Well, it's like this: Ms. Bontrager fooled me all the way—"

"As she did everyone," Liz hastened to add.

He nodded. "She was driving to town, saw me walking, and picked me up. Was I ever surprised, because I know she blamed me for the team's losing season. Then she said she was sorry everyone had been so mean to me. Said she was flying to Memphis to see the Grizzlies—Zach Randolph grew up in Marion, you know. They were

189

going to play Stephen Curry and the Golden State Warriors the next day. She offered to take me too—in her plane."

"Professional basketball stars," Caitlyn explained to Sadie. Liz knew Caitlyn had grown up in Marion, idolizing Randolph when he played high school basketball there. "I would have jumped at the chance to go."

He snorted. "You think I didn't? She had me meet her at the bus stop at four the next morning."

"After you'd stayed out all night," Sadie snapped.

Asher frowned.

Hush, Sadie. Liz joined the silent chorus from the other women. *If you want to fight with him, do it later.*

"Okay, I stayed out all night," he groused. "My friends from Fort Wayne came down. But after the movie, when they drove to the school to trash it, I talked them out of it."

So Chief Houghton's questionable witness had been telling the truth. Asher *had* been at the school the night of the break-in. Apparently he'd shown excellent judgment too. Much better than Ruth's.

"I knew you'd be mad." Asher glanced at Sadie. "So going to Memphis seemed like an even better idea. At first, it was amazing. I'd never flown before." After all he'd been through, his face still lit with wonder.

Liz shared a look with Sadie. *At least something good came from that rotten experience.*

His smile faded. "Then Ms. Bontrager said something was wrong with the flaps or something, and we'd have to land in Louisville. We'd still make the game, but while the plane was being fixed, she said she'd rent a boat and take me for a ride on the Ohio River." He snorted again. "She took me for a ride, all right. She wanted to show me the log cabin she and her family used when she was a kid. I was cool with that. Until she stuck a gun in my back."

A trapped-animal look grayed his bright blue eyes. "She chained me to a bed in the cabin. Didn't explain why she'd kidnapped me. Left blankets, food, water, and a pot nearby, but for days I wondered when she would come back. And what she would do. It seemed like forever."

As if given a signal, those still eating stopped. Kiera, usually undemonstrative, hugged him fiercely. Sadie gripped the table to keep from doing likewise. She muttered words Liz had never heard her say.

Mary Ann murmured, "Poisoning. Kidnapping. Stealing. I still can't believe Ruth did those things."

All grew quiet except the ticking of a mantel clock.

Then Asher broke the silence. "Never did care for cops. But when they broke down the cabin door, I was never so glad to see anyone in my life. It was the middle of the night, but those cops got a welder to break the chain." The big boy's eyes teared like a toddler's, and the room filled with sniffs and nose blowings.

"What will you do now, Asher?" Opal spoke in her understated but clear voice.

"Well, Sadie's brother lives near Fort Wayne. Says I can live there if I help farm."

"He's going back to school," Sadie chortled, as if she couldn't hold back one second longer.

Everyone cheered.

Asher rolled his eyes but grinned. "Yeah, I'll finish school there and apply to a community college where I can play ball. Maybe a scout will notice me, and I can transfer and play for a bigger school later on."

The conversation turned to college basketball, which Liz didn't understand. As opinions volleyed across the table, she slipped next to Asher and said, "I met your family when we were searching for you. What will you do about them?"

His chin dipped. "I'm not welcome there."

"I know." If only his mother could give him a hug.

Asher raised his head. "I'm going to visit them tomorrow, even though I may have to eat dinner at a separate table. When I was chained up, I told Gött that if He saw fit to free me, I would tell them I was sorry for hurting them. Because I am."

"Good." Liz patted his shoulder. The young firebrand had apparently learned some hard lessons during the past difficult months.

He looked past Liz, and his shoulders stiffened.

She turned to see the source of his tension.

Corinne.

The chatter in the dining room quieted again.

Asher stood and walked to her. "I'm sorry your father died."

Corinne's face paled, and Liz feared she would turn and walk away. After all, the kid had helped make Coach Albertson's last few months a nightmare.

Asher continued, "He gave me a place to live and taught me everything I know about basketball. I-I caused Coach a lot of trouble, and I'm sorry."

Corinne's dark eyes searched the boy's face as if x-raying his thoughts.

Liz held her breath.

"I forgive you." Corinne extended her hand.

Asher took it, his face crumpling. "Thank you."

Liz was sure her unspoken "Hurray!" echoed in all her friends' hearts. But no one knew what to say.

Kiera stood and took Asher's arm. "Sorry, everybody. But if we don't go soon, we'll miss all the fun stuff at school before the game."

"You're going?" Mary Ann said to Asher.

"Yep. Wish I could play. But I'll cheer the guys on. If they'll let me."

"If they hassle you, I'll smack 'em upside the head." Sadie shook a fist.

Asher and Kiera grinned as they left.

Naomi stood. "I owe you an apology too, Corinne. I suspected you were the murderer. I jumped to conclusions because Kate's my friend."

"I did too for a while." Liz offered her hand. "I'm sorry."

Corinne took Liz's hand, then reached for Naomi's. "How can I blame either of you? I wasn't exactly the loving daughter. I lost my mom when she was young, and I guess I always thought my dad and I would reconcile at some point. Then I lost that chance, and, well, I haven't been myself since I've been in Pleasant Creek. But the things you ladies and Kate did for my father really brought closure for me. Thank you. I can say goodbye to him now."

More apologies and thank-yous were exchanged among the group, and hugs, tears, and laughter reigned for some time. Liz wanted this moment to last forever. But the mantel clock's chime told her it couldn't. She stacked plates and whipped them off to the dishwasher. The others carried loads of dirty dishes to the kitchen too.

"You seem in a hurry, Liz," Sadie purred as she joined forces with Mary Ann to rinse plates. "Is that a new shirt?"

Her partner mimicked her tone. "You wouldn't have special plans for the game, would you, Liz?"

Is there no privacy in this town? Liz rolled her eyes. *Of course not. What was I thinking?*

A tinge of wickedness lit Naomi's face. "Liz, you didn't tell me."

Corinne dropped her usual serious demeanor. "Me either. And I thought we were friends."

"I don't have to tell anyone anything." Liz frowned. "WPCN probably announced it on the radio, along with the hog prices and trash pickup times."

"Why should they do that when the Pleasant Creek marryin'-and-buryin' grapevine is alive and well?" Caitlyn asked. "We all know you'll be going to the game with a certain handsome mayor."

Their smug smiles made Liz wonder if this unity thing was such a good idea after all.

"Jackson and I are just friends." The second she said it she knew it was a mistake.

"A *friend*, she says?"

"Oo-oo-ooh, yeah."

"Wish I had a friend with muscles like that."

Well, I always wanted sisters. Heat creeping up her cheeks, Liz couldn't help but laugh at their good-natured teasing. She shoved her tray onto the counter and stuck her hands on her hips. "Look, this isn't exactly candlelight and roses. It's a sweaty gym and fuzzy orange socks. Not to mention a gazillion people who don't know how to mind their own business."

Taunts and catcalls ceased, but Sadie and Mary Ann elbowed each other. What with the others' knowing grins, Liz was glad to shoo her helpers out the side door. She had a date to get ready for.

She donned her peach sweater and orange socks and fluffed her uncooperative hair. *Jackson, I can't believe you asked me to this game. I can't believe I dared to say yes.*

He had taken her to the parade last Christmas where their togetherness had caused quite a stir. This second very public outing would only reinforce the rumors. Liz tried to tell herself it wasn't a big deal. But deep inside, she hoped she wouldn't regret it.

23

Liz had been baffled by March Madness, but with one step through the door of the popcorn-scented, packed-to-the-rafters gym, she got it. And she was hooked.

A slightly off-key pep band blared a song that made her want to dance. Ozymandias the Owl bobbed from one corner. A wealth of orange flooded the bleachers, but brilliant blue, red, and purple splashed the mass of people. Liz estimated that the crowd numbered only several hundred. Yet as people shifted and roared, electricity sizzled like it was Times Square on New Year's Eve.

Head-to-toe tingles stood Liz's hair on end. She should have brought hair spray, used curlers, worn a hat. Already, the faces that filled the nearest bleachers had lit up with "the mayor's brought a date!" recognition. It spread through the Pleasant Creek group as if they were doing the wave. A few older ladies telegraphed the dreaded "Lord bless 'em" look that assumed she and Jackson had set a date.

She knew her face was reddening.

Jackson said softly, "That's what I like about small towns. People are really interested in each other."

Well, that's one way of looking at it. A big reason she'd moved to Indiana was to lose the "don't talk to me while I'm texting" city mentality. She straightened her shoulders and smiled. "Well, we'll never fall through the cracks here, will we?"

So what had seemed like walking a gauntlet morphed into a stroll together among friends. Liz and Jackson said hello to Chief Houghton, seated near a basketball hoop at one end of the gym.

Good. He'll keep things civilized. Sort of.

Mary Ann, wearing her original cheerleader outfit, talked to Principal Oaks on the opposite side of the gym. She bulleted the details of some plan with her pom-pom.

An after-game celebration, Liz guessed. As she followed Jackson to their seats, she waved to Caitlyn and Corinne, chatting several rows above the basketball court. Liz smiled to see them together; it was good to have friends. Maybe Corinne could make her peace with Pleasant Creek at last.

Liz spotted the Rohers and Pattons, friendly new guests who had arrived at the inn yesterday, sitting with the Kleins, Kellars, and Meyerses perhaps a dozen rows up. She assumed it was Jerry sitting beside Dorothy. An owl head covered his completely.

"Wonder how he got it to light up like that," Jackson mused.

Kiera, sitting in the cheer block, waved and yelled, "Hi!"

No Asher? So he'd decided not to come. Maybe it was just as well. Many Pleasant Creek fans harbored plenty of hostility toward him. If the team lost today, coming here would have been the last thing Asher needed.

Oh no. The band was playing the school song.

Jackson stopped in his tracks and started to sing.

Yikes! Liz almost ran into him.

She and that song didn't mix. But she stood still too, fumbling with the words until it ended.

Jackson pointed to their seats, two rows behind the team and Coach Clark. "One of the great things about being mayor—I get some of the best seats in the house."

He did have a cute grin. And a few freckles on his nose she'd never noticed before.

Conversation wasn't easy because the school bands began an unofficial loudness competition. Talking into each other's ears would only heighten the impression they were a couple. She noticed a few envious looks from passing women. *I'm at the event of the season, with the best-looking man in the room. Relax. Why not enjoy?*

When the Pleasant Creek and Delemont teams charged out of their respective locker rooms, the crowd's roar vibrated the walls. Liz gripped the shaky bleacher.

"They've stood for years. They won't collapse." Jackson crossed his heart. "I promise."

The players, skinny teen warriors, all wiry arms and legs, shouted as they ran drills. The Delemont team, however, looked smaller than the Owls. Liz's guests had predicted that Pleasant Creek, even without Asher, could defeat them, and Jackson affirmed that opinion, citing the home-court advantage as an added bonus.

His voice trailed off at the sight of Sadie entering the gym. He exchanged stunned looks with Liz.

Sadie? At a sectional?

Even more astonishing—she wore an orange cheerleading outfit. And led Beans in his matching sweater, booties, pom-pom hat, and orange curls.

Jackson clapped a hand to his head. "I've come to sectional games since I was a baby. Sadie has never darkened the door of this gym for a single basketball game. What's she doing here?"

The cheerleaders surrounded Beans, patting his head. Mary Ann, at last freed from her medical boot, darted into the group from nowhere. As the teams gathered at their benches, the cheerleaders hurried onto the floor. The group was going to do Beans's cheer.

Understanding hit Liz, and her eyes filled with tears. *Sadie's taking Ruth's place.*

They performed it better than before. The energy in the air supercharged even Beans, and when he bellowed his "Woof!" finale, that set the crowd to roaring again.

Principal Oaks grabbed a screeching microphone. "Before we sing the national anthem," he said, amid crackles and squeaks, "we hope our guests will join us in honoring the late Coach John Albertson."

The place quieted as if it were a church.

Corinne?

Liz could hardly believe her eyes as the coach's daughter walked steadily toward the podium. But she came to a dead stop about halfway across the court.

"Who's she waving at?" Jackson whispered, now that whispering was necessary.

"I don't know." Whoever it was, Corinne didn't seem inclined to move until that person joined her. She gestured again, adding a small but encouraging smile.

Finally, a petite figure edged toward her.

Kate.

Liz wished she could see the teacher's face.

Then again, I would cry and make a fool of myself.

Together they walked slowly to the principal.

Corinne took the microphone. "My father loved playing in this gym, on this team, for many, many years. He loved coaching your sons. He would have loved being here today, whether he won or lost." She fingered the mic that had mysteriously ceased its squawks. "I . . . just wanted to thank you for your support and kindness during this difficult time."

She offered the mic to Kate, who stood pale but composed. She shook her head.

Principal Oaks took it again. "And now, Asher Hilty, a former Pleasant Creek player, would like to say a few words."

Liz's throat closed. Jackson's eyes bugged.

A rustle swept through the gym as the blue-haired boy, hands stuffed into his pockets, joined the others. Gaze glued to the podium, he cleared his throat. Twice. "I-I . . . Coach and I didn't always agree. But he was a good man. He wanted the best for me and for all his players."

He raised his eyes. "Coach did a lot for me. But I messed things up for him and for my team. For a lot of people." He looked from Corinne and Kate to the visiting groups. "I'm sorry you have to hear this, and I hope none of you ever does anything as stupid as I did." He gestured toward the clump of Pleasant Creek players. "I want to tell you guys that I'm *really* sorry. I just didn't think." Now he turned to the home crowd. "But I'll try to do better from now on." His head dropped, and he stuttered, "I-I guess that's all I wanted to say."

As he handed the mic back to the principal, Corinne patted his shoulder. After a second, Kate did likewise.

Principal Oaks intoned, "Please stand and remove your hats in a moment of silence to honor Coach Albertson."

The momentary rustle as the crowd rose faded to silence so deep Liz heard Jackson breathing. *God, thank you for this moment.* Her gaze brushed Corinne, remembering when they were duct-taped and helpless in Ruth's van. Waves of gratitude to Kate flowed over her. *Thank you, God, that we lived to see this!*

All sang the national anthem, which ended with another barrage of cheers. The Pleasant Creek section broke into the raucous three-part "Orange!" "Ozy!" "Orange-and-black-and-orange-and-black" cheer they'd yelled at the Day of the Draw. The Pleasant Creek team spilled onto the floor and dragged Asher to their bench, yelling and bumping chests with the big boy who took his seat at the end of the team's bench.

Liz dabbed her leaky eyes, slightly mortified by her tears. "I'm sorry, Jackson. I can't help it."

"Hey, I'm trying not to cry too." His hazel eyes did look suspiciously bright. "No way Coach's death could have a happy ending. But this is about as good as it gets—unless we win state."

A deafening buzzer sounded. The orange-clad hometown boys squared off against the purple-uniformed challengers as everyone found their positions on the floor. The referee held up the ball, and Pleasant Creek's lanky young center poised to jump against his Delemont opponent.

From the beginning, Pleasant Creek led and their victory never really seemed in doubt. After all the hype, Liz didn't find the game nearly as exciting as the rest of the home crowd did.

"Just wait till tomorrow night," Jackson said after the surprisingly easy win. "Wildton won the earlier game against Blaketown. So we'll play Wildton for the sectional championship."

She didn't believe Jackson when he insisted the crowd could yell louder—but stepping inside the next evening, she ate her words.

For two hours, the teams locked horns. In awkward yet graceful choreography, strong young bodies ran, leaped, dived, collided, passed, and shot the ball. She found herself absorbing basketball through her pores. Liz joined in screaming at the referees as if they were her sworn enemies, shouting encouragement when the Owls looked tired on defense, sputtering indignation at Wildton's sneaky tactics, and shrieking with delight when the home team scored. When her traitorous throat grew hoarse, she stood and threw her hands up in ecstasy or raging despair, along with other newly mute fans. She even did the wave.

No wonder March Madness invaded the Hoosier State every year.

Hoops provided Indiana's best, cheapest therapy. People who lived in this largely rural, landlocked state couldn't run to the beach. No ski slopes like those in mountainous states. Instead, they vented their midwinter frustrations at high school basketball games.

For the first time in weeks, vitality coursed through Liz, purging her of the demons that had battled inside her. High school basketball therapy, snowball therapy—both kept Hoosiers going during the long winter months. She cheered hoarsely, hoping they made it to state this year, and then glanced to where Asher sat at the end of the team's bench.

He popped up and down like a human pogo stick, celebrating, consoling, and urging his team on.

"Whoa," Jackson marveled, "Asher's magic. They're playing ten times better than at any game this season."

Still, Pleasant Creek trailed throughout the game. A big red-haired kid ruled the area around the basket like a hungry T. rex. Smart as well as strong, he swatted the ball out of Pleasant Creek players' hands and seized every rebound, yet he collected only three fouls, with one quarter to go.

Asher stood still, arms clasped behind his head. Though Liz couldn't see his face, she read his hunger to be on the court. Then he bowed his head.

Are you praying, *Asher?* God didn't take sides in basketball games, Liz knew, but this sectional was so much more than a game for Asher, Corinne, and Kate. For the team. For the community. So she prayed too.

Three minutes to go. Time-out. Coach Clark barked at his troops. The band played the school song. As one, the crowd stood.

Boys scattered to their positions. One Pleasant Creek player heaved a long pass to his teammate standing in a corner. He caught it, aimed, and let fly. Three points!

Not to be outdone, a Wildton guard dribbled down the floor and attacked the basket for an easy layup. Two!

Back and forth. Back and forth.

"You can't just exchange baskets!" Jackson roared. "Defense! Stop 'em!"

They couldn't stop that muscled redhead under the basket, but they could shoot like marksmen. They could outrun him too. Liz noticed the redhead leaned over, panting, with every blow of the ref's whistle.

Pleasant Creek's smallest guy skittered past him and made an easy layup.

"That's my grandson!" bellowed the tiny old lady behind Liz. "Get 'em, Mason!"

The referee handed the Wildton player the ball. He passed it up the floor.

Liz's section shook as they chanted, "De-fense!" *Stomp, stomp.* "De-fense!"

Jackson grinned. "Well, maybe the bleachers might collapse."

"Who cares?" Liz flung back, stomping harder. "De-fense! De-fense!"

The bleachers didn't collapse, but the Pleasant Creek crowd did when the redhead cleared out his defenders and stuffed the ball into the basket.

Five seconds left. Score: Wildton, 62; Pleasant Creek, 61.

Pleasant Creek called its last time-out.

Please. Please. Liz scanned the faces around her and knew they were thinking it too. *Please. Please.*

The Wildton team crowded the Owl tossing in the ball. All except for the redhead, parked near the opposing goal. Somehow, the Pleasant Creek kid managed to throw it to the short, sprinting "David" of the tournament, little Mason, whose grandmother remained staunchly vocal with her support. "Goliath" raised menacing arms. Mason attacked and drove to the basket, barely getting a shot off before he hit the floor.

The ball perched on the rim for a breathless second.

And fell in.

When the final buzzer sounded, the noise of the crowd nearly blew off the gym roof. The bench emptied. The cheer block spurted onto the floor, followed by the home crowd, streaming down from the bleachers. Asher lifted Mason high in the air. Jackson lifted Liz. She didn't object; she was too busy hugging him and screaming.

For half an hour, Pleasant Creek completely lost its mind to March Madness.

61

———————— ///////////////////////// ————————

After Liz locked the back door and shed her coat, she glanced at the kitchen clock. Two thirty in the morning. She wandered through the inn. Jackson had been right. Her guests still appeared to be celebrating Pleasant Creek's sectional championship.

She'd loved every minute of the horn-honking convoy that drove around town, then to Mary Ann's farm. There a huge bonfire blazed, advertising to the world that the Mighty Owls had conquered the Wildton Wolves.

Having heard the school song umpteen times by now, Liz knew all the words. They still beat against her cranium like drumsticks.

Would she—could she—ever forget them?

She wouldn't forget the fun day with Jackson either. She smiled as she headed for her private quarters. But her footsteps stuck to the floor.

Liz glimpsed herself in the rotunda mirror and groaned. Pro teams sprayed champagne to celebrate victories. The Pleasant Creek tradition of shaking orange soda—orange "pop" as Hoosiers called it—had destroyed her hair and makeup and possibly her peach sweater. If Jackson ever called her again, she'd be amazed.

Hearing a key in the front door's lock, Liz turned to the foyer.

Corinne. She looked as tired as Liz. But she was still intact. How had her chignon escaped the orange-pop deluge?

Her lovely smile distracted Liz from embarrassment at her own appearance. Liz greeted her. "Want to wind down with a cup of something hot and not orange?"

"Thanks. But if I don't climb those stairs now, I'll never make it to the second floor tonight." She paused. "I would like to thank you though. You've been a friend when I really needed one."

"I hate to think of your leaving tomorrow." Liz really did.

"I do too, but I'll come back soon. Still lots to do, especially at my dad's house." Her voice turned wistful.

"You don't have to be a guest to come and see me. Come for coffee hour anytime. And maybe I can give you a hand clearing out your dad's house," Liz offered. "I'll bet some other Material Girls could too."

"I'd like that." The lovely smile again. Corinne said quietly, "But before we start serious cleaning, I've invited Kate to choose mementos from Dad's things."

"Good." Liz didn't know what else to say.

But Corinne didn't seem to expect much of a response. She spoke almost as if talking to herself. "I never thought I'd call Pleasant Creek *home* again. I'm glad I can now." As she climbed the stairs, she waved good night.

Liz's feet suctioned their way to her door. Her clothes felt glued to her skin. They *would* peel off, wouldn't they? Or would she have to soak, fully clothed, in a hot shower?

Craziness. Sheer craziness. And if the team won the regional championship next week, look out!

During March Madness, Pleasant Creek, Indiana, lost every vestige of its signature sanity.

But who in her right mind would live anywhere else?